When We
Someone Else

"There is the surface, and there is everything underneath" might be the motto of these 11 connected stories following the lives of students from a New Jersey high school into their 30s. . . . This cat's cradle of characters and storylines—in which intersections are sometimes fleeting, sometimes acute, sometimes permanent—deftly exposes the challenges, and terrors, of becoming an adult.
    —*Kirkus Reviews*

Groves' interconnected stories follow characters whose expectations for their lives stand in sharp contrast to their later realities. . . . Threads between characters are cleverly revealed throughout the collection, and Groves' 11 poised stories nicely balance wit with poignancy.
    —*Booklist*

When We Were Someone Else

Rachel Groves

Winner of the G. S. Sharat Chandra Prize for Short Fiction
Selected by Hilma Wolitzer

BkMk Press

BkMk Press
University of Missouri-Kansas City
5101 Rockhill Road
Kansas City, MO 64110
www.umkc.edu/bkmk

Executive Editor: Robert Stewart
Managing Editor: Ben Furnish
Assistant Managing Editor: Cynthia Beard

BkMk Press wishes to thank Rachel Mills and Dylan Pyles.

The G. S. Sharat Chandra Prize for Fiction wishes to thank Valerie
Fioravanti, Leslie Koffler, Linda Rodriguez, and Evan Morgan Williams.

Library of Congress Cataloging-in-Publication Data

Names: Groves, Rachel, 1979- author.
Title: When we were someone else / Rachel Groves.
Description: Kansas City, MO : BkMk Press/University of Missouri-
Kansas City,
    [2018]
Identifiers: LCCN 2018036380 | ISBN 9781943491155
Classification: LCC PS3607.R67835 A6 2018 | DDC 813/.6--dc23
LC record available at https://lccn.loc.gov/2018036380

ISBN: 978-1-943491-15-5

This book is set in Arnold Boecklin and Bookman Old Style.

Contents

For Jonathan, the most extraordinary someone I know

The stories in this manuscript are deftly connected by narrative strategies, while beautifully depicting the (sometimes fraught) emotional connections between various characters.

Although the whole, with its related threads and passage of time, offers the many pleasures of a novel, each story also stands satisfyingly alone. The writing throughout is crisp and fresh, often funny and ultimately moving.

I especially admire the complicated (and subtle) plot lines, the courageous display of emotion (without sentimentality), and the writer's abiding tenderness for the characters as they stumble through their lives.

—Hilma Wolitzer,
final judge, G. S. Sharat Chandra Prize for Short Fiction

Halfway House

M y parents are fighting in the bedroom again, firing words like *codependent* and *enabling* at each other, but I wouldn't exactly call these arguments World War III. Because compared to these arguments, World War III would be a damn relief.

My friend Margo, who just got her license, pulls up in front of my house and rescues me. We smoke cigarettes all the way to school. It's one of my two favorite parts of the day, that sliver of time between home and school or school and home when I'm off the grid. Flying under the radar. I don't have to think about anything but my cigarette and the open road.

Margo is my neighbor and best friend. We are bonded by proximity and a mutual lack of social connections. She's in eleventh grade—one grade above me—and is one of those early late bloomers, the kind who got all her woman parts first but couldn't figure out what to do with them. Also, she's smart but doesn't want anyone to know because she's practicing the art of awkward seduction and bad flirting. I don't have time for guys because I'm practicing the art of getting the hell out of Dodge.

"I'm going to get a tattoo," she tells me in the car.

"You're only seventeen."

"Details." She waves her hand. "James Nolan has a tattoo. If I get one, he'll want to go out with me. It will ink the deal, if you know what I mean."

James Nolan is the kind of guy who would lose an academic decathlon to my cat, whose name is Prime, after the prime number. But Margo doesn't care; she's not in it for the intellectual stimulation.

Iᴛ's Mental Health Monday, which means I have my standing weekly guidance counselor appointment. The counselor is what you would call sunny with no chance of rain; she's always looking for the upside. As in, she's *only* looking for the upside. She tells me I'm very together, comparatively. In other words, I'm okay, relatively speaking, given the fact, or considering. Considering my older brother is in rehab after trying to kill himself. Given the fact it took a total of two attempts before my parents finally admitted he was suicidal and sent him away, which begs deeper questions about denial, which I suppose is normal for this kind of thing. When a parent stumbles across knives and blood they see either suicide or experimental art. The first time, my mom chose art.

"A *C* in math," the guidance counselor says as she scrolls around on her computer. "How do you feel about that, Tess?"

"Depends," I say, "on which direction I'm coming from. In the alphabet, that is."

She gives me what looks like a staged smile and nods. She ran out of things to say during our first session, after Jonah went into rehab, so she usually just checks my grades and asks me how I feel about them. The grades are a measure of my mental functioning, and her asking me how I feel about them is a measure of her ability to counsel me.

"Okay," she says, turning toward me. Now it's time for the closing arguments, the pearl of wisdom. "This is improvement. But you could be doing better. Right now I'd say that you're underachieving."

I'm not sure what to say. "I'll think about doing better."

"That's a demonstration right there," she says, expertly scaling the upside. "It means you are very smart."

I know what it means, lady, I could tell her. It means I'm smart in theory, stupid in application. It means I used to be smart when I could do long division in my head. When I could sweep a competition at Mathletes, back when I cared about things like Mathletes. It means I shouldn't have flunked math. It means I should have never gone on academic watch, which sounds weirdly close to suicide watch. As if failing math and failing life were somehow equivalent.

At home, after school, the air feels iced over. Mom is in the bedroom with the door shut. Dad's still at work. They probably had another fight on the phone, or she talked to my brother, who gets to make a phone call once a day. She naps a lot, after fights or getting bad news, both of which are usually about Jonah, like his stay in rehab getting extended, again. There are times I want to tell her that she should appreciate me for being a pretty good kid and not going into a rebellious frenzy while she sleeps. I could be running a meth lab in the basement, and she'd never know it. But I hold back on playing that card; I need an ace up my sleeve just in case.

Margo comes over, and we listen to records on the old record player in Jonah's room. Mom cleans his room every week, even though he's been gone for a month. As if a clean room will suddenly make him want to live. I wonder if my mom and guidance counselor both checked the same *Sunny-Side Life Manual* out of the library.

Margo paints her nails while I scratch my name into the bedpost of Jonah's bed with a butter knife. Not my real name but my nickname, Sloopy, the one that Jonah gave me. I'm leaving a message for him, a secret goodbye for when I run away.

"So, are you coming or not?" I ask Margo, dragging the knife around into an *O* shape, which is harder than an *L* but easier than an *S*. "Because I'm serious about freedom."

Margo looks up from her nails. "What about your brother?"

"He can come when he gets out. *If* he gets out. I heard that someone at school knew a guy who was in rehab for seven years."

"Tragic. I'm just worried that leaving might ruin my chances with James Nolan."

"I'm pretty sure your chances were ruined by not existing."

"I guess we both have problems," she says, starting on her second coat of nail polish. "Let's drown our sorrows in alcohol."

It's not a bad idea, considering. With my mom in a nap coma, I could easily sneak a bottle of wine out of the kitchen, no problem.

But I still have another *O* to scratch out, which could take a while.

"Just think about the whole freedom thing," I say. "Let it marinate."

I finish the first *O* but it looks less like a circle and more like a defunct polygon.

On Saturdays, I get to visit Jonah in rehab. We sit in the common area of the facility while my parents wait outside so we can have sibling alone time. The common area looks like an old living room that was donated from the sixties. The room connects the various units for the various conditions: trauma, drug and alcohol, eating disorders, and teens. Apparently being a teen is a condition serious enough to have its own ward. Jonah got admitted on a triple combo pass: trauma, drug and alcohol, and teen. I'm not exactly sure what counts as trauma, but whatever it is, Jonah seems like he's got it. He looks colorless and flattened, like he's been getting smacked in the face every day.

I watch all the strung-outs and low-lifes wander around like zombies. I could totally be a drug addict, if it wasn't so clichéd. I say *clichéd* because that's what people expect from me, the younger sibling. They expect me to either go the mental freak-out route or to totally bail and become straight edge. But straight edge is just addicted to not being an addict, and isn't that really just an addiction of another kind?

"I miss you, Sloopy," Jonah says to me, trying to smile. But his eyes get all lazy when his mouth turns up, like trying to smile makes him immediately fall asleep. Like it's impossible to be happy, so it's better to sleep. He obviously gets that from our mom.

Sloopy is the nickname he gave me when we were little, and I would fall asleep in his room listening to records. When he tried to wake me up, I'd say, "But I'm sloopy." The name reminds me of things that are from before and that are never coming back, like me and Jonah hanging out in his room, so I hate it when he calls me that. But even more, I hate it when he's not around to call me that.

"How are things?" he asks, playing with a cigarette he's been holding. In designated outside areas, smoking is allowed, I guess because it's not the worst thing the patients could be doing, relatively speaking. I want to ask him if we can go to the designated outside area so I can bum a cigarette, but my parents are right outside, and I'm pretty sure that being on academic watch hasn't earned me a free smoking pass.

"Things are fine. Please don't ask me about math."

"Okay," he says, laughing a little as I work up my nerve to ask him something.

"Jonah?" I say, softly, trying to land my question without crashing.

"Uh huh."

"Do you still want to die?"

He looks at me, not smiling, which means his eyes are not droopy at all, but awake. He sighs. "Sometimes. But I'm trying not to want to."

"Is it because of drugs?"

"Yes and no," he says. "Drugs are a problem, but they're the problem on top. There's another problem underneath, which is the real problem."

I want to ask him, is the problem that there is a problem underneath or is the problem underneath *the* problem? But I'm not sure if that would solve it for me.

"He's doing okay, don't you think?" Mom asks when visiting hours are over. She's trying to be positive which makes me feel like I'm having another non-conversation with my counselor. I could shatter Mom's world with one word, but instead I say, "Yes, comparatively speaking."

On the car ride home I complete the rest of my answer in my mind like a worksheet:

Compared to a prisoner of war, Jonah is doing great.
Compared to the President, not so great.
Compared to a millionaire, pretty bad.
Compared to me, question mark.

Margo let the whole freedom thing marinate. We work on our plans to run away in her room, where we listen to CDs since she doesn't have a record player. I like being at Margo's house, for the quiet, for the oppositeness to my house, which is always nuclear. But recently, the quiet at Margo's seems more quiet than usual. *Too* quiet. Margo's parents never fight, but now they've stopped talking at all, which somehow seems worse. Like a sneak attack is coming.

"First, where will we go?" I ask her.

"My aunt has a house upstate. It's a summer home. She's not there in the winter. We could go there."

"OK," I say, calculating. "What about when the summer comes?"

"We'll go somewhere else. We can take my car."

I shake my head. "They'll find us in two seconds."

"How?" she asks.

"License plate radar satellite technology. They can find kidnappers from space."

I think I'm making that up, but Margo won't question it. Her investigative skills, if she has any, appear to be completely dormant. She takes things as they come. I envy her for this.

"You're right. Besides, my parents will want the car back. We'll take a cab. Do you have any money?"

I shake my head.

Margo mulls this over. "Tell your parents you need money for Spirit Week—say you need to buy a costume or something. I'll do it too. Then we'll have some money. We can get jobs when we get upstate."

It's a terrible plan, but it's the only one we've got, which makes it the best one we've got.

"When do we leave?" she asks.

I skim my mental calendar for my availability.

"Thanksgiving," I say. "For the irony."

Over the next two weeks, Margo and I are even closer than usual. We are bonded by our secret, what no one else knows, the power in all that we could do. Suddenly things don't seem to matter as much because we're so close to clocking out. We've got a bad case of short-timer's disease.

On Thanksgiving morning, I layer up in my running-away clothing, just in case it's colder upstate. My suitcase is packed and ready to go. My plan is to sneak out my window and meet Margo between our two houses, where the cab will pick us up.

I figure it's time for goodbyes. I give Prime a goodbye pet. If he's broken up about it, it's hard to tell. Next up: my parents, although it won't be an actual goodbye, obviously, just an any-last-word type of thing. The kind of thing that, later, when they think about it, will become retroactively packed with all kinds of meaning.

I find Mom in the kitchen, basting the turkey.

"Well," I say, not quite sure what these last words should be. "Things could get real interesting around here."

She nods as she sucks up the turkey juices in the baster. "Yes, it will be nice for the four of us to be together again," she says.

"The four of us?"

Suddenly she's beaming. "Your brother is coming home on Saturday! I didn't want to say anything until we knew for sure."

Just then I feel our plan, Margo and my perfectly flawed plan, crumbling like my mom's banana bread. In no way can I leave now. Not when Jonah is coming home.

I retreat to my room and call Margo to let her know that our plan must be postponed indefinitely. She's pissed but she doesn't hang up on me, which means she's not that pissed. Maybe I'm not that pissed either.

Now that Jonah is home, everything is different. For one, no more Mental Health Monday. I get the clean bill of health from my guidance counselor who has somehow succeeded because our family unit is complete. For two, my parents stop fighting. Instead, Mom spends most of her time in the kitchen making meals that include a meat and a boatload of side dishes that are mostly variations of the same thing: peas and carrots, carrots and onions, onions and peas.

But now that Jonah is home, nothing is the same. Jonah spends most of his time on the porch smoking cigarettes, writing in a journal, and not talking to anyone. Or, he's sleeping. On Christmas morning, I try to wake him up super early to go pounce on Mom and Dad, our ritual since forever. But he just sleeps and sleeps, like a baby. Or like the dead.

Jonah's eighteenth birthday is just before spring. We throw him a party, but he doesn't invite any of his friends because they're into all the old things he's no longer into. He's not supposed to hang out with them or even see them. He's not even going back to school. Mom and Dad have decided he will finish senior year at home.

It's still pretty chilly outside, but Jonah wants to smoke, so we bundle up and have the party in the backyard. Mom and I set the table, and Dad serves up hamburger patties on buns. Jonah is awake, which means he's smoking.

We sit quietly for a while, munching on burgers and chips and beans and potato salad.

"How's that job hunt going?" Dad asks.

Jonah doesn't answer him. He's not eating really, just picking at his food.

"Gotta learn how to be a productive member of society, kiddo."

"Do you really think referring to me as kiddo is appropriate, considering?" Jonah asks.

Exactly, I agree, but silently of course.

"It's important that you follow your after-care treatment plan," Mom says quietly. "We don't want you to slip."

"Don't throw your glossary of recovery terms around at me. You have no idea what this is actually like."

Jonah lights up a cigarette, takes a few drags, and ashes into his plate of food. After the longest silence, Mom gets up and goes inside. Dad and Jonah just sit, staring at each other, replicas. Both have the same thick, blond hair, broad shoulders, and hard looks. But if Jonah's look is steel, Dad's is even stronger. Finally, Dad gets up and follows my mom inside.

Jonah lights up another cigarette. I could crack a joke to break up the silence, but I don't. This feels like the ocean, and I'm afraid of an undertow.

Mom and Dad are standing at the kitchen window. She washes dishes while Dad stands next to her, talking. She is crying. He looks angry. They are fighting again.

Dad moves to the other end of the kitchen, and Mom turns toward him, like a face-off. Now Mom is angry too, fighting back through the tears. Their hands move around like a pantomimed fight, like marital-issue charades. Some sound escapes through the door. Now they are both screaming.

I imagine what they could be arguing about. Jonah's after-care treatment plan. My underachievement. Being enabling.

Suddenly they both stop talking and just stare. It looks like a draw. Maybe they've agreed to just kill each other mercifully. Then Dad makes a face, the goofiest face I've ever seen. It's so out of place that it's wrong, offensive even, like someone laughing hysterically at a funeral. I'm sure my mom is gonna blow her top and throw a plate at him. She should. But instead, she starts laughing. Then he starts laughing. They look like two clowns. They are the comic relief in their own tragedy.

MARGO picks me up to go to a party in the next neighborhood. She's in a dress I haven't seen before, one that shows off her curves. I've never gone to a party before, and Margo has only talked about going. I figure the fact that we're going means that she's forgiven me for not running away, but I can't be sure, because we don't talk about it. It makes me feel like we're Margo's parents.

"Everyone's going to be there," Margo says, in a new, aloof voice. "So you have to play it cool, Tess."

Ever since Margo's parents stopped speaking she seems strangely hollow. She's like a hologram of Margo—from this angle she's cool party girl, from that angle she disappears into thin air. Vaporized.

At the party, Margo and I are completely out of our league. But Margo's hologram doesn't care about leagues, and she's in charge. She zeroes in on some senior guys and strikes up a conversation.

I tag along because I have nowhere else to go.

"Hi," a tall senior says, suddenly next to me. I'm surprised to find it's James Nolan. I glance at Margo, who's occupied with her guys. "So what's your story?"

"Mostly underachievement and foiled plans to run away," I say. "It's a memoir."

He doesn't really get it, so he starts talking at me about football and the new engine on his truck, jumbled boy-talk that interests Margo more.

Then he slides in closer to me as if our relationship is already moving to that next level. Being this close to James Nolan sets off a deep, sparkly feeling that surprises me. Still, something feels out of place and potentially dangerous, like I left an appliance on somewhere.

Suddenly, James grabs my waist and pulls me toward him. He smells like beer and potato chips. The sparkly feeling short circuits. Then, across the room, I see Jonah. Jonah! I'm surprised and relieved, like I'm being rescued from a ship I didn't know was sinking. I don't even care that I'm elbowing a senior—*James Nolan* of all people—away, causing him to curse out loud, which, in turn, captures the attention of Margo, who shoots me a double-sided look: one side anger for screwing with her burgeoning reputation and the other side sadness that it's happening through James Nolan. This is most likely social and best-friendship suicide, but considering that I've faced actual attempted sibling suicide, this is just a stroll through the teenage drama ward.

I head in the direction of Jonah, who is standing in the corner with a couple of other kids. Kids he didn't invite to his birthday. I slow down, my good luck fizzling out as I remember to wonder what he's doing here. I don't know all the post-rehab rules, but I'm pretty sure he's on social parole. I check his paraphernalia from afar: a cigarette and a water bottle. That's okay, considering. Still, I get the feeling he's not supposed to be here. And I'm not supposed to see him here.

I beeline for the front door. I can make the walk home. Margo's hologram will be fine, I tell myself.

I DON'T tell Mom and Dad about the party but instead watch how things play out over the next few weeks. Jonah finally gets a job as a night cashier at the Shop Rite. My parents seem content, but I'm still worried about him slipping. Clearly it's up to me to make sure he keeps it together. I cultivate a plan around keeping an eye on Jonah.

There are two challenges to keeping an eye on Jonah. Challenge number one: when he goes to work, he is out of my sight. I will address this by riding my bike down to the store and sneaking past him with a cart. Then I will stand in aisle two and pretend I'm indecisive about soup. Really, I'll be watching him at the checkout counter to make sure he doesn't do anything fishy, like leave early or take too many bathroom trips. I will be like a secret shopper, browsing the mental health of my brother.

Challenge number two: Jonah's journal. He writes everything in that damn journal. I'm convinced there are secrets in there, secrets to keeping him on his after-care treatment plan. Since he's mostly at work or at home, the only way to get a look in that journal is when he goes to work.

After spending some time prioritizing, I decide to tackle challenge number two first. When Jonah leaves for work, I slip into his room, which looks like he tossed a grenade in it and walked away. Even so, I don't have to look hard for the journal. It's right on his bed stand. It's a plain brown leather journal with a tie. I pick it up.

"What are you doing?" Mom's at the door. I'm caught red-handed, a journal-thief, stealer of private thoughts.

"Nothing," I say, putting the journal back.

"It's hard not to worry about him, isn't it?" she says. "He's been having a tough time."

You're telling me, I want to say.

"It's probably time to tell you that Jonah is leaving."

"You're kicking him out?"

"No, he's *moving* out. His decision. It's too hard right now for him not to slip." She sits down on the bed with that look, but I don't know if what's coming is just a little water on the face or a tsunami. "He's going to live in a halfway house."

Tsunami. A tsunami is what was coming.

"You mean that place where addicts live? Like a frat house for addicts?"

"Sort of," she says, and she looks like she's trying not to smile. "Hopefully without the frat part."

"But how will that be better?"

"Being out of rehab is really hard. Life after rehab can be jarring. Recovery is messy. The halfway house will be a better place for him to transition."

Transition from where to where? And how will living with a bunch of drug-addict losers help him get from wherever that is to wherever that is? The thought of him leaving again makes me feel defeated and circular, like I'm stuck in an endless loop.

"This is all your fault," I say, finally. "You're so enabling."

I storm out to leave her alone with Jonah's private thoughts.

Margo has a boyfriend she met at the party. He sits with us at lunch now. He's not James Nolan, but he's someone, which is all that matters to Margo. He's a big jock who's all hands, all over her. He's an accessory to all the new things she wears now, low-cut tops and tight jeans, short hemlines, hairspray. Hologram Margo is really kicking it up a notch in the skank department.

"Do you wanna come over and listen to records?" I ask her at lunch.

"Me and Nick are going to the lake. We're gonna meet some people."

"People?" I raise my eyebrows. "As in lake people? Is that like swamp people?"

"Be cool," she hisses at me.

Nick glances at me, suddenly aware I'm there, although *aware* seems like a strong word for this guy.

"Hey, you're that girl who pushed my friend," he grunts.

"Hey," I say coolly. "You're that guy whose friend put his hands on me. Which means maybe I should push you too."

He's three times my size, but he obviously didn't expect that one. His expression goes blank. "I'm gonna get a soda," he says.

"Why do you have to be so weird?" Margo asks angrily, after Nick leaves the table. "Nick gets me."

"Please. He gets that he can touch everything under your shirt."

Margo's face turns pink, then red, then back to normal. "Whatever. People are saying things about you. That you're in Loser Town. It's probably time to tell you that me and Nick are going to sit with his friends from now on. Since clearly you don't want us here."

"Have fun," I say. "Don't get pregnant."

Now that Margo's moved out of Loser Town, I take the bus to school and listen to records in Jonah's room with Prime, who, it turns out, is not much of a music lover. Mom and Dad are back to their usual fireworks show, lighting each other up with accusations and screaming at the same time for the grand finale. I'm back to working on my plans to run away, only without Margo.

After arguing about it for a couple of weeks, Mom and Dad finally agree to let me visit Jonah at the halfway house.

Dad drives me to the place, which is a forty-five-minute drive downtown. All the way there I try to imagine what a halfway house looks like—half-prison, half-soup kitchen, maybe. But it's just a regular house with two stories, a staircase, and a living room with a TV. Not bad, considering this is where a bunch of addicts are holing up.

Jonah comes downstairs, and I can't quite decide if he looks good or not. His skin has gotten darker, and his hair has grown out a little. He looks better than rehab but worse than life after rehab.

I meet Timmy T., a guy in his forties who looks like he's had it rough. He chain-smokes and wears shirts with no sleeves. He's got a homemade tattoo on each shoulder, an eagle and an American flag.

He tells me and my dad, "It's tough man, it's just tough. War isn't hell. War is war. Life is hell. You got to do what you can. You got to just take it day by day. Minute by minute. Smoke by smoke."

He's fought in some kind of war, and I want to say "Preach it man!" For the patriotism. But I don't have enough nerve, and really, I can't say I know what he's talking about.

"I'll be close by," Dad says before he leaves me with Jonah. "If you feel uncomfortable, you call me, and I'll be here in three minutes flat."

"Please," I say rolling my eyes. "It's just a halfway house."

After Dad leaves, Jonah and I take a walk downtown. We eat ice cream cones while window shopping.

"It sucks without you at home," I blurt out between licks of mint chocolate chip.

"It does?"

"Yeah. Mom and Dad are so codependent. They screw everything up. I wish they'd just get it over with."

"Get what over with?"

"The divorce."

Jonah doesn't say anything. I want to ask him if Timmy T. is going to be his lifelong friend, like Margo used to be mine. I want to ask him if he is transitioning better. I want to ask him if he's coming home.

But I suspect that if the answers to those questions aren't *no*, then they aren't *yes* either.

Back at the house, Jonah shows me his room, a small, square space that he shares with Wendell. Wendell's drug of choice is crack, Jonah tells me. Wendell has been to rehab three times. He's been sober for almost a year, but he lost custody of his kids. If he wants to see them, a social worker has to be there, too. They don't get to come over unattended like I do. I'm suddenly ready for my dad to come pick me up.

"Hey," Jonah says, after my dad pulls up on the other side of the street. "Go easy on them."

"On who?" I ask.

"On Mom and Dad."

"Why?"

"Because it's a big job, being a parent."

"Compared to what?" I demand.

Jonah lights a cigarette and shrugs. "Compared to nothing."

Right then I feel as if I'm being kicked from the inside, like something is trying to get out, and the only way to get it out is just to have someone, for once, say exactly what everything is compared to everything else so I know where things stand.

"How can you compare something to nothing?"

"Because not everything has a comparison. It's not all relative to this or that. A lot of things are just hard, in and of themselves."

I get in the car with Dad and we pull away as Jonah waves goodbye to me. I guess now that he's eighteen he's officially an adult. But there on the street in front of the halfway house, he still looks as freaked out and small as a kid.

MARGO no longer has a boyfriend. It seems that he found out about her hologram, that her popularity was just some kind of a trick with light.

We sit and eat lunch. Margo's wardrobe has returned to its regularly scheduled program.

"My parents are getting a divorce," Margo tells me. Her face is blank, and it's hard to tell how she's taking this.

"Well that's good, right? You'll be happier."

She stares at me for a long time. Too long, like she has a reaction so big she's trying to talk herself out of it. Then her face gets flushed, and her lips get tight, and I feel like I know what's coming.

"What the hell is wrong with you?" she asks.

I feel bad for saying that. But I'm not sure what I've said exactly.

"Anyway, I'm going to live with my dad at the end of the school year," she says, not looking at me. "Upstate."

"Why?"

"My mom's gone schizo. She can't deal."

"But, I thought they couldn't stand each other? Isn't it what they wanted?"

"It's not that simple."

"Yes it is. You either want to be married or you don't."

"I think there may be something in between."

"Something in between?" I repeat. Like Jonah, between kid and adult. A laugh, between two fighting parents. A house, halfway between rehab and life after rehab.

"Do you know what I mean?" Margo asks, and I can tell she's not asking because she wants me to understand, but because she really, really, needs me to.

"Sort of," I say truthfully. "But not really."

"Me too," she says.

At home, I find Mom in bed, taking a nap. I want to wake her up and tell her that Jonah is not transitioning well. That it's better if he comes home. But I don't know that it is.

So I climb into bed and curve myself around my mom, who's sleeping on her side, wondering if this is what it's like to be a parent, with a job so big you just want to sleep. If I had to boil it down, I would say that a parent's two main jobs are trying not to get divorced and keeping their kids alive.

But I don't know if that's all of it. And that's the problem. And if that's not all of it, I don't know what the rest of it is, which means I don't know what I don't know. And that's the problem underneath the problem.

I do know that all the idle mental threats probably aren't helping anyone.

So I tuck in close to my mom. "Don't worry," I say very quietly. "I won't start a meth lab in the basement."

It's quiet for a minute before I hear, "Good to know."

I rest my head against her back in that space in between her shoulders and listen to her breathe. I want to tell her one more thing: that she's doing a pretty good job, because Jonah and I are still alive, which is a great thing, just in and of itself.

But I can tell by the way she's breathing, she's already transitioned back to sleep.

The Person at the Window

THE PERSON AT THE WINDOW

The Valley Hill Apartments in South Jersey had enough problems with dilapidation and property neglect; now the Tuesday-night news was reporting that two female tenants had seen an unidentified man around ten o'clock the night before, peering into their bedroom windows while they undressed.

An indirect sense of violation invaded Amelia as she listened to one of the victims, who lived just one building over, describe the perpetrator as *just plain tall*, which happened to be the exact phrase Amelia used to describe her husband, Lucas.

Whatever terrible thought was insinuating itself into Amelia's mind needed edging out. Lucas worked nights at the coffee shop, she reasoned. He was accounted for. Amelia turned off the TV, closed the dirty, plastic blinds and dialed him at work to prove her point.

"What do you want me to do about it?" he grunted loudly after she relayed the neighborhood news. "I mean, he didn't actually *do* anything to anyone right?"

"But looking *is* doing something," she said, at a strange loss to explain what seemed obvious and feeling stupid for calling him. He was right; what could he do about it while he was foaming lattes and digging lemon bars out of a display case? She hung up, double-checked the lock on the front door, and returned to the couch, where she forced her concentration into finishing Add Up Your Total, an exercise for her first-grade math lesson plan in which students helped the lunch lady Miss

Pickle, whose cash register had broken, by completing eleven simple addition problems that didn't require any carrying. Creating these worksheets eased her mind; she liked to think she was laying the cornerstones of critical thinking that would later lead to important milestones in a student's life. It was a minimal but rewarding existence, this being a teacher. Amelia might have preferred more reward and less minimal, such as being a mother. And an actual career for Lucas. And a real home, like the one that Lucas had promised they would be moving into any time now for four years.

The idea hadn't died—ideas never died with Lucas but were just endlessly reworked. "If we can get a no-money-down loan we could finance the whole thing," was the latest iteration of the home-owning plan, augmented by actual drive-bys, in their shared Camry, of the houses they could possibly live in for no money down. Looking at houses was a kind of substance of things hoped for; all of the dreaming and planning and what-color-paint seemed closest to creating kinetic energy when they drove up curbside to a house for sale and imagined themselves living there—with kids. Lucas wanted a lot of them and quickly; this expressed desire had wooed Amelia, among other expressions. When she first met him he was hauling around a GMAT study guide and looking at law schools. He would graduate, pass the bar, and she would quit teaching and have babies. But after they married and moved into Valley Hill, the law-school-related literature was never unpacked from the box in the closet. She kept working. He thought about working. Eventually the small sum of money her parents had given them as a wedding gift dwindled to nothing, and he was forced to take the coffeehouse job while figuring out life-after-the-pursuit-of-law-school.

She found herself in bed by nine-thirty as usual but staring at the ceiling awake and clutching at her chest in the dark, as if wrestling some truth to the mat, trying to force a tap-out. Sometime after eleven she was still awake, aware that her husband had come home and was standing in the doorway to their room, removing his shoes. Then climbing into bed with her, reaching for her with his oversized hands, groping in the dark. Then his mouth over hers, followed by his body—lean, broad shouldered, six-five, dwarfing almost all of her, save for the words *just plain tall* that were now coming back up in a most vomitous way.

AMELIA watched the news avidly every night for two weeks, waiting for any updates. But all was quiet on the voyeur front. It was a fluke, she decided. A random, passing crime. She was being paranoid and ridiculous, which, quite frankly, was an enormous relief. She felt a safety valve close off in her, one that clamped down a near-nuclear fear.

There were other reports, other stories that interested her. As long as the news featured these, the valve could remain shut, the looming question could just suffocate and die.

She started to become a little fascinated with the news.

"Remember that weird girl in school who always wore black?" she asked her friend Frank, who she now called almost nightly to give a report. "She was an underclassman when you were a senior. Sally Krum-something? Well, she's running for Mayor."

"No way. That batshit-crazy girl?" he said. "Didn't she do something weird with a dead animal?"

"A squirrel, I think," Amelia said. "I vaguely remember. But yeah, who would have thought *that* girl? Oh, and that hit-and-run victim died yesterday. And there was another robbery at the 7-Eleven on Jackson."

"Why do you keep watching that stuff? It's depressing."

"It's important to be aware of what's happening in your community."

Frank was a friend who'd graduated in the class ahead of Amelia at high school. They'd reconnected at a creative writing course at the local community college over the summer. "I'm nurturing my creative side," she had told him after they recognized each other. "So I can nurture my students' creative sides."

"That's so precious," Frank said. "I could puke."

O<small>N</small> Friday afternoons, Amelia joined other teachers for happy hour at a local chain called Eat Eats, a big, family establishment with a gigantic and excessively themed menu arranged in categories called First Eats, Small Eats, Big Eats, Sweet Eats. The happy hour drinks were called Liquid Eats. The place had various pictures on the wall of food-consuming patrons they featured as Eat Eaters.

The teachers spread out across high-top tables at the bar, where alcohol was consumed at a rate Amelia felt was slightly alarming for elementary school teachers; as if drinking to round off a hard edge was counterproductive to the gentility required in molding young minds.

"You're so lucky you teach in a non-testing grade," said Teri, a third-grade teacher who was sitting next to Amelia. "On top of their regular subjects, I have to get them prepared for standardized testing. Concentration has gone out the window. Suddenly they're all problem children."

Amelia sipped on her mai tai, a ridiculously ornate drink with at least half a pineapple stuck on the rim, and thought about Evan, an energetic but sometimes distracted boy who might be considered a problem. Earlier that day she had assigned self-portraits as a creative way for the kids to discover how they see themselves. They were allowed to draw in any style—realistic, impressionistic, abstract—as long as they felt it represented who they were. Even if the concept was a little advanced, Amelia thought this was the kind of seed that would be planted into their young soil, later producing a garden of self-aware adults.

But Evan had sketched a picture of an older man with brown eyes and a beard.

"Is this your father?" she asked, crouching down beside him.

Evan looked straight at her with his big blue eyes and nodded.

"This is very good, but this is supposed to be a self-portrait. This should be a representation of you."

Evan made a small frown and scrunched his nose. "My mom says I'm handsome."

"You are handsome. That's why I want to see a picture of *you*. Can you try again?" She drew a sheet from the pile and placed it in front of him.

He seemed momentarily resistant, staring down at the fresh piece of paper. But soon he set his pencil to sketching, and Amelia relaxed, her confidence in the process restored. Just a minor hiccup, too trivial to mention to Teri, who was going through glasses of wine faster than usual.

"Enough about work," Teri said, clearing the air with one hand. "How's your husband? Lucas, right?"

"He's doing great," Amelia said, nodding, a small twitch starting up in her leg, like a dog being scratched in a spot somewhere else. "He's practically on a management track at work. Knowing him, he'll end up running the place."

She was forced to look away from Teri who seemed apt, any moment, to start asking prying questions. A big family shuffled into the main dining area. Waiters pulled chairs together to seat the entire group, which totaled seven kids and two exhausted parents.

"Lucas and I are really getting into a groove," Amelia added to the quiet space between her and Teri, not even knowing what she meant or why she said it. But not saying it would have left her half-dressed in the conversation, with Teri curiously peering at exposed skin.

"How is your husband?" Amelia asked, out of obliged reciprocity. She was still watching the family.

Teri shrugged and stared into her glass of wine, shoulders slumped. "Honestly, we're not doing so well."

"Teri," Amelia looked back at her, thrown off by her transparency, "what's going on?"

Teri looked at Amelia with soggy eyes. "It's just hard. We've been together twelve years, and it's just hard."

Amelia tried to imagine twelve years with Lucas. The past four years, times three. Three times the amount of part-time work, three times the amount of video gaming, three times the amount of pseudo house-hunting that was making her close to giving up and just moving into a cardboard box. She was a patient person, she felt, but had she been waiting far too long?

She went back to observing the big family, who was spiraling into dining chaos. One kid had disappeared under the table, another one banged silverware on the table. Two others were crying. The parents had that exhausted, shackled look—chained up and checked out. *Lucas and I won't have that look when we have children*, Amelia thought, the twitch starting again, the word *when* itching in such a far off place that reaching for it seemed a waste.

On Saturdays, Amelia met Frank for lunch at a deli, a weekly tradition that had carried over from the summer. Amelia had invited Lucas once, but his dismissive refusal made her feel guilty in some way and after that, lunch with Frank went unacknowledged.

"How's the community doing?" Frank asked.

"Like you care?" Amelia countered, opening up Boxed Lunch #2, her usual, a turkey sandwich, potato chips, apple, and chocolate chip cookie. Opening the neatly folded, cardboard box produced the tiniest burst of release every time, as if she were relieved to find everything was in the same place, as it should be.

"Are you kidding? I care so much I've developed an ulcer. Two, in fact. Both bleeding."

Amelia ignored him and unwrapped her sandwich. Frank was known for his unrelenting sarcasm—he was a movie critic for an alternative city paper and was paid to be judgmental, to seek out the flaws, to uncover every imperfection.

"So, what do you have going tonight?" he asked.

"Nothing. Lucas has to take the car to work."

"Why do I even ask? When are you going to get two cars like normal people? Forget that, when is he going to get a full-time job like normal people?"

"He's almost full-time. Anyway, it's just an interim job."

"An interim between what? Lazy and super-lazy?"

Amelia took a bite into her turkey and mustard on rye. Maybe she could eat this conversation away.

"Can I be honest?" Frank asked, picking at the roast beef that he always ordered and never ate. Frank lived on coffee and criticism.

"Is there another choice?" she asked, chewing.

"I think you've got a big, fat problem," he said. "I think he's a big, fat sponge, and you're a big, fat body of water."

She swallowed. "But he's my husband. We're supposed to share."

"What you're doing is not sharing. What you're doing is letting him mainline your blood supply."

"Gross," Amelia said. She picked up a chip and crunched on it, trying to shove the image of her giving Lucas a blood transfusion out of her mind. Usually, she found Frank's unapologetic starkness oddly likeable, but today it rubbed too close to the bone. Still, she considered him as one of her only friends and had even thought about planning a double date with Frank and his wife Sara, an ex-model getting her master's in French studies, but the idea seemed barren before she even suggested it to Lucas. He preferred fighting interstellar battles in Halo with a six-pack of beer. What could she expect of a loner who had practically been orphaned—no father he knew of, a mother who lived across the country, and an estranged brother Amelia had never met, who had not even been invited to the wedding.

On Sundays, Lucas printed off a list of addresses from his online search and drove Amelia beyond the cheap apartments and deteriorating duplexes to a tree-heavy subsection with multistory homes and three-car garages bigger than their apartment.

"What about that one?" Lucas pulled to an oversized, two-story, stone house with extensive landscaping.

"We can't afford these," she said, head against the window.

"We could with no money down," Lucas said. He drove to another house for sale on the next street over.

She knew about these homes—her sister Joanna lived here with her wealthy new boyfriend. Amelia had been over once, before Joanna's life was filled with successful friends and better real estate. These homes had big, sun-lit kitchens with stainless steel appliances and granite countertops. Living rooms with winding staircases. Plantation shutters. Lawn guys. The kinds of things they could not afford, even for no money down.

"Well?" Lucas was asking. "What do you think of this one?"

The house that Amelia was staring at came into focus: a brick house with a wraparound porch, lots of windows, and a gigantic red oak in the yard. "It's too expensive," she said again, the words deflated before they cleared her mouth.

"I'll bet we could get a loan with your credit," he said as she stared at one of the second-story windows, that woman from the news now a ghosted image behind the glass, the words *big, fat problem*, piling themselves onto this moment like a shovelful of dirt.

Evan had redrawn his portrait as a woman with blonde-brown hair in tight spirals all over her head. But the eyes were what startled Amelia; they were a dark green that was almost black—huge, round, absent eyes.

"Is this your mother?" Amelia guessed.

Evan nodded.

"This is very good. But this should be a representation of you. Do you want to try again?"

"This sucks," Evan said, crossing his arms.

Amelia put her hand on his shoulder, even though there was a strict no-touching rule at school. She felt that a small touch could have a calming effect, assure Evan he could discuss his feelings, and thus lead to constructive conflict resolution. "What is making you so upset?"

"This sucks! Suck sucky suck."

"That's not a word that we use in this classroom. Do you want to go in time-out and take a breather?"

"Time-out sucks."

She pointed to the time-out chair in the corner of the room, a gesture that pained her. No child in her class had been sent to time-out this year.

He reluctantly got out of his seat and went over to the chair, where he planted himself and then made faces at the other students.

She sighed and made a note to discuss this issue with his parents at the next parent-teacher meeting.

"I started going to a marriage group," Teri told Amelia at happy hour. "You should come with me."

Amelia squinted at her, a little rum-fuzzy. She was on her third mai tai, two more than usual.

"Why do you think I need to go to a marriage group?" she slurred.

"Because you have that look on your face."

"What look?"

"The look of a married woman."

Amelia agreed to go, if only because it gave her something to do. The next Wednesday, Teri picked her up and drove to a house in the same neighborhood as Lucas's imagined future neighborhood. It was a big, three-story house with nineteen-foot-tall ceilings. The entire house was decorated from floor to rafter with Oriental rugs, crystal knickknacks, framed pictures, gigantic window treatments. A woman named Patty lived there—a sturdy, big-boned woman who had been married for fifteen years to a rosy, round man with the same enormous grin in all of their pictures.

Have an open mind, Amelia told herself, as she took her seat in the circle of women in the living room. The faces around her looked generally content and surprisingly normal. This is what Amelia felt like she had looked like, before the inside of her got tangled, making her face distorted and jumbled in the mirror. Maybe good old-fashioned married-woman talk was just the sorting-out she needed.

This particular evening was pet-peeve night. Every wife was supposed to share a pet peeve she had with her husband.

"My husband leaves his dirty glasses all over the house. By the bed, in the bathroom, out by the pool," one woman exclaimed.

"My husband used to do that too," Patty said. "So I stopped washing them. Pretty soon we ran out of glasses, and he figured it out."

A few more women shared their pet peeves—bad table manners, never throwing out junk mail, snoring in front of the TV—and others chimed in with helpful solutions. It appeared that the general format of the group was validation and problem solving. Normally, Amelia would have liked the idea, but all the affirmation was unnerving her.

"We haven't heard from the new girl," Patty said. "Do you want to share a pet peeve?"

The women turned toward Amelia in unison, as if she was going to give a brilliant speech. Amelia blinked at the expectant faces. *For a minute I took my husband for a voyeur*, she thought. But said, instead, "He always leaves his shoes in the middle of the floor. As if he simply walks out of them," she said. "I hate that."

"Oh, yes," was the general murmur of the crowd.

"Same problem at my house," one woman spoke up. "You know what I did? I put all his shoes in a pile in the living room and said, 'If that's where you want your closet to be, that's where it will be!' He stopped leaving his shoes there after that."

The women nodded. Amelia smiled courteously and wondered how in the world she could have just lied through her perfect teeth.

"WHAT's your marital pet peeve?" Amelia asked Frank at the deli on Saturday.

"We haven't had sex in four months. Super annoying."

"Oh," Amelia said, blushing a little. "I'm sorry."

"Forget it. Let's talk about your terrible marriage. What's the deal with pet peeves?"

"The marriage group was discussing pet peeves, but I lied. I said he leaves his shoes in the middle of the floor. He doesn't do that. That's the one thing he doesn't do. Why did I lie? And it's not a terrible marriage."

"You're in a marriage group?"

Amelia stared at her untouched lunch. She hadn't meant to tell him that. Especially after promising herself she would not discuss her marriage with Frank. But she couldn't help it—admitting the truth was an influx of air she needed, like some sort of emergency tracheotomy.

"Yes, I am," she said, emphatically. "And I'll tell you a real pet peeve. He told me that after we got married we would travel to Europe. He even bought three travel guides. They're in a box in our closet. We would take our love on tour, he said."

"How insufferably trite," Frank said, whose own boxed lunch had been torn apart, picked at, and played with. "Not to mention ridiculous. He had what, five dollars in the bank? And it was your five dollars."

"That's not even the half," she was saying before she could stop herself. "Do you know how many almost-careers he's had?"

Frank shook his head.

She counted off on her fingers. "Lawyer, wedding photographer, real estate agent, musician. At one point he was going to own a nightclub. Then it was a computer business. The list goes on. Every time, I thought, *this could be it*. I fell for it *every* time."

A tangle of dormant truths loosened in the pit of her stomach, the word *voyeur* dislodging itself slightly. Was this something she could mention to Frank?

"Well, whose fault is that?" Frank asked, leaning forward against the table.

"What?" She blinked at him, *voyeur* slithering back into the dark pit.

"Whose fault is it that you fell for it? He said the words. But you chose to believe them."

She drove home, wondering if it was true, that it was her fault. Lucas was still asleep when she got home. He slept in late on weekends, probably during the week too, she suspected, although she had never verified. Never wanted to verify. He seemed capable of living a life so separate that maybe they had never even met at all. Was that her fault? She felt as if she was outside herself, knocking against her skull like someone at the window, demanding an answer. *I don't know*, she said to the person at the window. *I did everything the right way.* Good grades in school, no intravenous drugs, a career that could make a difference. So maybe getting married after five months had been a little reckless. But Lucas had made her feel like the missing piece to his puzzle, the sexy bow on top of his grand ideas. When he reached for her, she felt wanted, his big hands pulling her head back and kissing her deeper than she had ever been kissed.

But maybe, she thought, it had been too deep. Too sexy. He seemed wrapped up in her in a way that had nothing to do with her—always running his hands roughly through her tousled auburn hair, grabbing at her small waist. But avoiding her eyes, as if she was just the centerpiece to some imaginary charmed life.

And there were traits, there were mannerisms, there were certain truths about him that bothered her. Sleeping into the afternoon. Hours of video games. A juvenile response to adult problems. And sex—she was not always sure that consent was as necessary to him as it should have been.

But she had taken a vow. And she believed in the power of the marriage vow. You took a marriage vow seriously. You held up your end, and the other would be raised up; it would have to be. And she hadn't exactly been holding up her end. She never cooked, never cleaned. She spent more time taking care of her students than taking care of her husband and their home.

Holding up her end could start with meals. It could start right now. She was starving from not eating lunch anyway. She pulled a pound of ground beef from the freezer, dug some potatoes out of the pantry. Flipped to a recipe in a low-fat cookbook she found under the sink and carefully followed instructions for meatloaf and healthy mashed potatoes with oil in the place of butter and chicken stock instead of whole milk. A healthy, delicious, responsible meal.

When Lucas finally woke up she was setting the last of the dishes out on the plastic kitchen table they hadn't eaten at together for over a year.

"What's going on?" he asked groggily.

"A meal," she said, steering him into a seat. "I'm going to start cooking. We are going to start eating together, every night. I'll prepare meals in advance so when I get home from school, we can heat it up and eat before you go to work. No more every-man-for-himself. What do you think?"

"Badass," he said, picking up his fork. "I'm starving."

"And laundry," she said, sitting down, pulling a napkin over her lap. "And cleaning too."

After he went to work she separated all the laundry by color, made piles that went in the dryer and piles that got line-dried. Followed care instructions to the letter.

Then she dusted and mopped and dusted some more. She cleaned the blinds. She arranged his video games in alphabetical order and ironed his barista aprons. On Sunday afternoon, she cheered on his video gaming and was first in the car for house hunting. Later that evening she practiced what she taught her kids and painted her self-portrait—an oval, petite face with brown eyes, an understated, closed-lipped smile, and soft, brown curls.

Afterward, in bed, she made the first move, pulling Lucas toward her and kissing him, slowly, stroking her fingers against the back of his neck softly. He pushed into her immediately with a force that used to be exciting, one she equated with intensity and passion. But now she imagined there was just a moment of delay between her call and his answer, the small possibility that he wanted to give instead of just take.

"WHAT, may I ask, in the hell are you doing?" Frank asked her the following Friday night. He was standing in her apartment with a glass of wine, viewing her drawing like he was in a gallery.

"I'm holding up my end of the bargain," Amelia answered, from the center of the couch. "I'm being a good housewife." She swirled the wine around in her glass. She had been a good housewife—for a good solid week. In celebration, she had invited Frank over for a glass of wine. Now that his wife was spending all of her time in the library, his evenings had become mostly free.

"The person in this painting looks vaguely horrified," he said.

"That person is me. I'm content. It's my self-portrait."

"It makes me think of some kind of existential hell."

She finished off her wine and poured more. The booze was giving her a sense of certainty and courage. Certainty that her husband was not a pervert. Courage to turn things around in her marriage.

"Tell me," Frank said, wheeling around to face her, "if this is your end of the bargain, what's he holding up?"

Amelia thought for a moment, then raised her glass, a toast to nothing. "His high score in Halo," she said.

AFTER a four-week hiatus, the voyeur was back with a voyeuristic vengeance, spotted three days in a row. Witnesses all corroborated that he was extremely tall and broad shouldered.

Amelia sat on the floor in front of the TV, frozen. A cop was now patrolling the area, but she was absolutely terrified. This felt bigger than anything the police could solve, a personal impending doom that made handcuffs and Miranda rights seem like kids playing at cops.

She crawled backwards onto the couch, where she lay awake and waited for the ten o'clock news, hoping to hear that he had been caught, that he was the old man next door, or the teenager with the loud car stereo.

At just past ten, Lucas came through the door. "What's up with the cop outside?"

She stared up at his looming figure in the doorway, feeling helpless and small.

"They're trying to catch that Peeping Tom."

"Oh," he said, avoiding her eyes. He disappeared into the kitchen and returned with a beer.

"Do you mind?" He motioned for her to move. She sat up and shifted to the left. He flipped on the gaming console and sat down. She stared at him while he started working the controller, perched on the edge of the couch, as if she wasn't there. She wondered how many times she had been relegated to watching this permanent profile, a face to the TV, just one half of him showing, the other half always obscured.

"You're home early," she said slowly, the words, like boulders, rolling out of her mouth with enormous effort.

He kept his eyes forward, not moving, not blinking. "No, you're up late." And the way he said it made it seem like some ironclad truth she dared not question.

"Sᴀʀᴀ and I are getting a divorce," Frank told Amelia at lunch.

"Oh my God," was all Amelia could say. She hadn't ordered Boxed Lunch #2. She had lost her appetite.

"She's been seeing some French photographer. They're moving in together."

Amelia stared at Frank, who was actually eating his sandwich, almost happily, as if everything was normal. Better than normal. It was a defense mechanism. She knew, because she was guilty of it too. She made healthy mashed potatoes and had sex with a man who hadn't said he loved her in forever. The truth was, marriage was just one nasty bait-and-switch, a faulty try-and-buy.

"You know what I think? I think marriage is false advertising," she said, watching roast beef disappear into his mouth. "We should sue the institution of marriage."

"You're edgy today. What are you going to sue for?"

"All those promises. Those things he said he would do. I invested in those promises. They were my stock; now they are worthless lies. If I can't have what he promised me, then I want my money back."

Frank smiled, a rare occurrence. "Who are you?"

She looked at him. "I'm Miss Pickle. And my cash register has broken. I need to add up my total."

That evening after Lucas went to work, Amelia walked around the apartment and imagined all the things she never got. Flowers Lucas never bought her, the broken garbage disposal he never fixed, the video games he bought instead of the pinstriped chair from that consignment store she loved. Those damn video games. Plastic containers full of things she never received from him—time, attention, frugality. A working, responsible husband who contributed to society.

She lugged a box out of the back of the closet and dug out its contents—a study guide for obtaining a real estate license that he never got, an expensive and unused video camera that she had saved for months to buy him for his wedding videographer business, books on starting various businesses. There were so many potentially lucrative jobs he failed to obtain that it was impossible to add up the total. The value of those promises simply couldn't be determined—the carryover would be immeasurable.

"What are you doing?"

Lucas stood in the doorway.

"Cleaning," she said, not realizing how late it was.

He came into the room and sat on the bed, took his shoes off. He went quiet behind her. She wished he'd go away. But then his thick fingers were dragging their way through her hair. Startled, she leaned forward, jerking away from his reach.

"What's wrong with you?"

"Nothing. I'm just not in the mood."

She detected a distinct drop in temperature, like crossing into dark, unknown territory. She turned around.

He was leaning forward, glaring at her. "Is this about Frank?"

"What?"

"Are you having an affair with him?"

Amelia stood slowly and crossed her arms. She was at his eye level. "No."

"Don't you see him every week?"

"He's my friend."

He grunted. "Just don't have an affair with him."

She locked eyes with him until her vision was tunneled and it was just his eyes, untethered and floating. They had always been this way, hadn't they, eerily detached and everywhere.

He pushed off the bed and clomped out of the room. She surveyed the items strewn on the floor. These were just relics of the problem that resided in that top layer of rock. The real problem was underneath. Nothing was what it seemed—and she wasn't so sure that she didn't already know that. And if she did know it, if she did know that nothing was what it seemed, did it mean she was in on it?

AMELIA met with Evan's mom, a middle-aged woman with overly permed blonde hair, during parent-teacher conferences on Tuesday night.

"Evan is a bright young boy," Amelia said. "He has so much energy. But, he's a little combative. And he seems to have picked up the word *suck*. Is that a word you use at home?"

Evan's mom held her purse in her lap, as if she was just about to leave. "Probably got it from my ex. He only sees the kid one weekend a month, but he seems to have more power over him than Christ."

"I see," Amelia said, measuring her words carefully. "Well, you might want to sit down with him and find out if something is upsetting him."

Evan's mother let out an exaggerated sigh. "Look, you're the teacher. It's your responsibility. It's your job to teach him."

"It's my job to make sure he learns basic skills," Amelia said, feeling feverish. "But it's not my job to parent. We both need to work together here, for the best interest of Evan."

"Don't talk to me about *best interest*," she said, leaning over her purse. "I'm a single mom with four kids. I'm doing what I can just to make sure they eat. You do think eating is in their best interest, right?"

Amelia nodded numbly as she stared at those chemically produced curls and two gaping holes for eyes, amazed at Evan's accurate representation of her.

THE marriage group was discussing romantic date night ideas. One woman recommended a picnic in the park, with a basket of his favorite things. Someone else suggested a candlelit dinner and a sexy massage.

Amelia thought it all sounded like a brainstorming session for one of those pornos made for women. She didn't want to talk about romantic date nights.

"I have a pet peeve," she said, when the conversation hit a lull.

"Well," Patty said, tucking her legs under her chair. "We're not on pet peeves tonight."

"That's OK. I still want to share."

Patty glanced around the group at their nods. "OK," she said.

"I've never met my husband's brother. They haven't spoken in almost five years. You know why? He told me that his brother's wife accused him of coming on to her at a party, and after that they all stopped speaking. Lucas claims he didn't do it, that she was a crazy bitch who was in love with him. I didn't believe him. But I didn't know that at the time. Can you not know something that you know?"

"I believe that's called denial," Patty said quietly, her face a pale pink. "But I hope he didn't do it."

Amelia glanced around at the group, who looked absolutely mortified, like a pregnant animal had given birth to a litter in the middle of the room, and every baby was stillborn and rotting.

Then she looked back at Patty, who was staring at her feet. "Well, for fuck's sake," she said. "Me too."

FRANK invited Amelia over to claim any clothes that Sara had left behind when she moved out.

Amelia sorted through a pile of items Frank had thrown into the center of his guest room.

"Her style is prettier than mine," Amelia said, holding a beautiful silk flowery dress up against her shorts and T-shirt.

"Stop it. You're a knockout," Frank said.

Amelia put the dress down, surprised. "That's the nicest thing I've ever heard you say."

"Don't make a scene."

She tossed the dress back in the pile.

"Hey, did you hear?" Frank said, then sipped his coffee for a moment. "Sally Krum-something got elected. The paper did an article on her."

Amelia imagined Sally getting ready in the mirror, smoothing out her navy suit jacket, fluffing a freshly cut bob. A politician's bob. The kind of haircut that indicated she was dependable, predictable, safe. Then, opening up her sock drawer, where she reached into the back to stroke the dead animal she kept in there—her dark, ugly secret.

"All these people who are somebody else," Amelia said, her lip trembling. "Nothing is what it seems." Frank nodded, his brow wrinkled. She noticed, not only was he handsome with thick, dark hair and a strong jaw, but that she had quietly pushed this fact away many times before. Maybe they *should* have an affair. That's what Lucas thought was happening anyway. Then she could at least make something what it actually seemed.

"I think Lucas might be the Valley Hill voyeur," she said.

"The who?"

"The guy who's looking into people's windows at night. They named him that after the Valley Hill apartment complex. I think it might be him."

"What are you saying?" Frank said, sitting down next to her.

"I don't know," she said. Every artery inside of her felt like it was being snapped, one by one. "What do you think would be worse—that he's *a* Peeping Tom or *the* Peeping Tom?"

"Is there a distinction? If he's one, isn't he the other?"

But she couldn't answer. Instead she helped Frank take Sara's things to the Goodwill bin around the corner, and then she drove home, just in time to hand off the car to Lucas, who hadn't talked to or even looked at her in a week—a cruel, calculated punishment for rejecting his advances. She then sat at the window until it turned dark. The cop was not patrolling tonight. She thought about those women who had been violated in their homes. She wondered how many had been violated without knowing it. And she wondered if she had been one of them.

At half past ten, she saw some movement outside the building across from hers. It was a person, moving along the vinyl siding, avoiding the street lamps. He crouched just outside of a window and peered in. She watched him commit this sickening act for several minutes. Then suddenly, he stood up and turned in her direction. She pushed up close against the glass, squinting as hard as she could. He was definitely tall, broad shouldered—it certainly looked like Lucas. Then again, who could tell? Everyone looked the same from faraway. It could have been Lucas, but it could have just as easily been Frank. It could have even been Patty, who was tall and broad shouldered herself. A realistic Lucas, an impressionistic Frank, an abstract Patty, as if everyone was just a version of someone else, a different representation of the same portrait. She turned away.

But what did that mean for her sister-in-law, a woman she never met but had dreamed of, a faceless victim, a mute scream in the dark? And how many other victims would there be if a face was not put to the crime, a face that was exactly what it was? Amelia turned back to the window. The man had stepped toward the street and was now partially in the light. He was half visible now. Amelia no longer wanted to see, not like this, not in part nor in secret. She glided toward the front door, hurried down the stairs, and walked straight toward the man, who stood half in shadow, half out. As she got closer he pulled away from the light and walked along the building. When she reached the light under which he'd been standing, she stopped. In a week, when she would file for divorce and move out of the filthy apartment, she would remember this moment, just before she called his name and made him turn, how she already knew who it was, how it was already impossible not to know everything from where she stood in the light.

Smells Like Leslie Gray Martin

Smells Like Leslie Gray Martin

If popularity were an atmosphere, Leslie Gray Martin would live in the exosphere, the highest layer around the earth. If popularity were a video game, Leslie Gray Martin would have reached the highest level after defeating the dragon, finding the keys to all locked doors, and turning every stone into coins. She is a shining example of all that can be accomplished with just a little hard work and perfect genetic makeup. She is a beacon of hope to the underprivileged, underclassed, underinvited. It has been said by her classmates that Leslie Gray Martin is a terrible force; underneath that flawless skin and teeth like white plantation houses she is one lip-glossed raging bitch.

What am I but the lowest of lows standing here in the school cafeteria, a troll with an awe so tall it can only cast the darkest shadow, that shadow of my secret desires, like kidnapping Leslie Gray Martin and putting her in my trunk for safekeeping. And also for asking about beauty tips. *Hello*, I would say to the Leslie Gray Martin in my trunk, *you are my best friend. We will be together forever. Please remember you have no choice in the matter, as you are tied up in my trunk. And also, your hair is lovely. How do you get those curls so soft? What's that? The secret is sleeping all night in rollers? You mean that's not a perm?*

It's this kind of thinking that leads me to think that Leslie Gray Martin could be from the future, sent back in time to show us the way. For example, perms are currently very in. All the popular girls have perms. All the popular girls except Leslie

Gray Martin, that is. Her hair is a darkish brown with blonde highlights, and it cascades to the middle of her back in loose spirals that keep their curl in a soft, un-chemically bound kind of way. I can't imagine a time without perms in it, but clearly Leslie Gray Martin knows something we don't. She has seen the future, and she knows.

About the trunk thing, please let me clarify. I'm not going to kidnap Leslie Gray Martin. I'm not a pervert or a psychopath or a general danger to myself or to others. I'm just finding my voice, like my therapist tells me to do. *Find your voice* and *live in moderation* are the two things she repeats at every session. Sometimes I try to find my voice by looking for it under the couch or in the back of my closet, but trying to live in moderation is a little trickier. I do this by going to extremes in my mind so as to find my way to the middle, where moderation is, and hopefully my voice.

And this is one of those times like when you're learning to ride a bike, and all you can look at is the tree in front of you, and your dad is yelling at you to look away or you will hit the thing you are looking at, as now I am walking directly toward Leslie Gray Martin's table with my lunch tray until I am mere inches from her, where I stop, staring. Her friends gawk with disgust. But Leslie Gray Martin stares back, expressionless.

"You're Leslie Gray Martin," I say, thinking immediately, what have you done, Sally Krumbert, this is exactly like looking God in the face and checking his I.D. at the door, you dimwitted nimrod. You don't check God's I.D., and you certainly don't look him in the eye. You just let him in with no questions asked.

"That's funny," she says. "No one calls me that. Who are you?"

"I'm Sally," I say, and I have to do everything in me, and I mean everything, including kicking myself under my internal table, if you know what I mean, to stop myself from saying: *Sally, like the mustang, like Struthers, like* Smokey and the Bandit, *like Leslie Gray Martin's best friend in the whole world.*

"Are you a freshman?" she says, tilting her head, examining me, but examining what, it's hard to say.

I nod and think, *Dammit, Sally Krumbert, why wouldn't you at least falsify your age for a little credibility here? Be a little smart. At least say you're a sophomore.* Then again she'd probably know I was lying with that extrasensory internal lie detection radar that she most likely possesses, and then I would have really blown any chance at getting more face time with Leslie Gray Martin, so I keep nodding, thinking, *Dammit, Sally, you are smart, good job at spontaneously telling the truth.*

But now I'm staring and nodding and staring and trying to find my voice, but I can't, so I make this little gesture toward the table.

"You want to sit here?" she asks, like she's guessing my charades, and I think *Oh no, Sally, you just asked to sit with Leslie Gray Martin without asking to sit with Leslie Gray Martin. That is not your voice, that is not your voice.* But she shrugs and moves over.

Now this is quite an unexpected turn of events. So unexpected one might be looking at a few possible unexpected reactions, such as shouting her name to the cafeteria, peeing my pants, sobbing with joy, or, for that slightly more physical expression, form-tackling her onto the floor. But I suspect none of these things will serve as confirmation to Leslie Gray Martin that she made the right decision by accepting my non-verbal request, so I clamp myself down as fast as I can on the bench so as not to reverse current circumstances through any kind of mitigating reaction.

But now I have the very serious problem of containing my sheer excitement. No, of containing the spectacular fireworks of emotions that have already reached some kind of grand finale in my chest. I might vomit a sparkler at any moment is what I'm saying.

Other popular minions join the table and fire off looks of disgust, confusion, sheer disbelief—or cross-versions of these—disgusted confusion, confused disbelief.

But Leslie seems unfazed by her peers' reactions. Bored, even, by her supporting actors. She eats her lunch, chewing, not speaking to me or anyone else, though others seem to be trying to get her attention. Maybe she's forgotten I'm there, and I will be left to slither away like some garden snake to the edges of that vast, dirty lake that is high school, where I will submerge myself until my eyes are at water level, watching this lunch table in remembrance of the five most glorious minutes on earth, when I walked on land with the mammals.

"So. Sally," she says, as she picks at her turkey sandwich. "What are you up to when you're not in this lame-ass place?"

Now this is an interesting question. One that seems to be an inquiry that may be part of a larger survey on how the lower social class actually lives outside of school—do we clock in at the child-labor factory that mass-produces sparkly headbands and neon scrunchies or do we simply return to the cave from which we crawled? Are we regularly starved and beaten by our parents? Or maybe she's just interested in minute, but important, details like how my cereal must have exactly the right amount of milk or how sometimes I pet my cat extra hard when I feel nervous.

"I'm pretty boring," I decide to say, finding now that I too have picked at my own sandwich in a kind of sandwich-picking shadowing technique. "I usually just take the bus home and hang out."

"Ah, the bus," she says. "The bus sucks."

I'm nodding in agreement which means we're having a moment where we're sort of even, but that makes me feel sideways, so I say this: "You could give me a ride home after school today."

Now she's looking at me with a look. The complex look of Leslie Gray Martin, one that you can't describe or understand or even draw, which I sometimes try to do, when I'm home, alone, and I want to see her face.

"Aren't you a funny one?" she says, tilting her head. "Where do you live?"

"Timber Oaks."

"I live one neighborhood over. I could give you a ride, I suppose."

If I had a ring, I would propose. Not in a romantic, same-sex-marriage kind of way, but in a simple life-long-commitment-to-best-friendship way, just to firm up this tentative offer she is making to me.

"Okay," I say, almost too fast, almost laughing, almost slapping myself in stupendous wonderment of such a moment that just, cannot, be happening.

"I'm parked in the far lot. It's the blue convertible. You can meet me there after eighth."

I know the blue convertible, the chariot of the goddess. I've ridden it in my dreams. I've bedazzled it with our monogram, S&LGM. But I say all of this under my internal table, of course, where I am jumping up and down with joy, bumping my head repeatedly against the hard surface of myself.

BETWEEN lunch and eighth period it's like this: slow, painful, torture. Like sleep and food deprivation, like waterboarding (which I don't know what it is, but it sounds terrible) combined with bamboo shoots and electrocution. Basically, I have to take a hall pass in every class and go to the bathroom, where I sit in the stall and clench my fists and close my eyes until the feeling passes, that's how excited I am. Because if I don't do that, I will burst into a million pieces, and there will be no way to get those pieces into Leslie Gray Martin's blue convertible in a way that is not a huge, annoying mess. So I hang on as best I can until eighth, and when the bell rings I tear out of school and force myself to slow down into a kind of fast walk/almost jog, lest I appear overeager, toward the far lot.

She's not there yet, probably because she is not doing a fast walk/almost jog but more of a regular walk/non jog, a stroll-through-the-lilies-of-the-field type of thing. Plus, she has to say goodbye to her twenty thousand gazillion friends who are all trying to get time on her calendar that's booked at least six months in advance at all times. Except for today, in which apparently there was an opening—perhaps that person got shot, which would be unfortunate for that person but serendipitous for me, sorry to say. Either way, I'm on that calendar.

Eventually I see her coming across the field—a small dot and then a medium-sized dot and then a full-sized dot in the shape of Leslie Gray Martin. She climbs into the car, which has the top down, because, of course, that's what you do with a convertible. You have the top down and climb in it. Which I do too, and now we're both sitting here.

She checks herself in the mirror and then starts the car, and we take off. It's windy and loud, which means we can't talk, but Leslie Gray Martin seems okay with that. The wind billows her silky blouse, and her hair swirls about like some animated halo, her scent of brownies and laundry and popularity making its way toward me. Meanwhile, my black sweatshirt clings to my body, and my thin frizzy hair, too fragile for a perm, frizzes out even more until I look like Leslie Gray Martin's Frankenstein pet that she's taking for a ride.

Leslie Gray Martin turns on the radio. It's the Boyz II Men song "End of the Road," and I want to turn it off, as this message seems contrary to my very purpose right now, metaphorically speaking. And also literally speaking, as now that I am sitting in Leslie Gray Martin's blue convertible I certainly don't want to come to the end of any road.

She sings out loud, flat and sharp all over the place. I know exactly which places are flat and which are sharp because I myself am actually a good singer, having been in choir since fifth grade and now in the freshman choir, where I've secured the coveted solo spot in the Spring Recital. I suddenly feel the urge to share that fact with Leslie Gray Martin, although I'd have to yell it, and that seems not quite the information she might want yelled to her at this moment. Plus, she's really getting into the song, so I figure, if I can't beat 'em, and I tap my feet too and hum along, and it's like me and Leslie Gray Martin have our own little two-person singing group.

We wind around the road toward my house, passing thick woods on either side. I imagine us building a shack in those woods and living there alone, forever, like forest creatures of the best-friend species. Maybe we could walk on all fours and pet each other before bed each night, and one of us (her) could put a leash on the other one (me), but *No*, I hear my therapist saying, *live in moderation*. So I change the fantasy to a nice apartment instead over on Main Street where we are roommates who have popcorn movie night every single night.

"Smells like Teen Spirit" comes on the radio. Leslie Gray Martin turns it way up. This seems curious to me; the darkness of the song now seems contrary to Leslie Gray Martin's purpose, which is to spread a message of hope and rainbows across a devastated teenage land. But she's singing along to the verse and the chorus and the verse and the chorus: "I feel stupid and contagious/here we are now entertain us." She knows every word.

It dawns on me that maybe this is her attempt to bridge the gap between us, that she imagines this is how I feel, *stupid and contagious*, because why wouldn't I, and by singing this song she's saying, *Hey, I understand, I know you feel this way, and you're not alone—not because I feel it too—in no way do I feel stupid and contagious, but I know you feel this way and now there is at least someone in the world who knows you feel this way.* And I guess we're having a moment with this song. So I start singing along too—loud—louder than Leslie Gray Martin to say, *yes, I hear you hearing me on feeling stupid and contagious.*

The song ends just as we pull into my neighborhood. I navigate her down the streets to my house, where she pulls the car up to the curb and throws it in park. Up until this point I didn't plan on what would happen next. The thought of having Leslie Gray Martin in my house, while it propels me into a state of euphoria that can only be compared to receiving a lifetime supply of mint chocolate chip ice cream while the news announces that homework has been cancelled, officially, across the globe, also sends me into a state of sheer, unadulterated panic. There are so many things that have not been prepared for her arrival, including bleaching the house from top to bottom, touching up the paint on the crown molding, melting the sherbet in the ginger ale punch, heating up the hors d'oeuvres, drawing a bubble-bath should she choose to take one, installing the soft lighting, and the complete gutting out and renovating of my room, both functionally and aesthetically. But now she's here, and there's no time for any of that.

"Oh," I say, trying to sound totally impromptu. "You should come in."

She leans forward and looks at the house, as if assessing whether the structure is worthy to hold her, temporarily speaking, of course. Then in one move that makes me nearly soil my pants, she cuts the engine.

She follows me into my house, which, thank my lucky whatever, is empty since my parents are both working—a fact I don't mention because I don't think two working parents is something you want to advertise as I'm sure Leslie Gray Martin's parents are both at home, lounging by the pool and drinking cocktails while their money makes more money, which is what my dad tells me the rich do for a living.

"Are you hungry?" I ask, dumping my bag on the counter.

"Um," she says, as she wanders into the living room, looking at our stuff. It's ordinary stuff, but I suspect she finds it interesting because of its sheer oppositeness to her house, which I imagine is filled with roller coasters and cotton candy.

I root around in the fridge, cursing my mother under my breath for not stocking up on assorted after-school snacks. We've got cheese, pickles, juice, mayo—not the kinds of food that can make other food that can be eaten. I find a slice of chocolate cake left over from last night.

"I have some cake," I say, but Leslie Gray Martin is standing at the far end of the living room looking at a big family photo my parents forced me to be in last year. We're all wearing red shirts because it's Christmas, which means we're supposed to look like Santa.

"It's just you and your parents?" she asks.

"Yeah," I say, trying to figure out what to do with the cake. Present it to her on a silver platter and feed it to her bite by bite, perhaps.

"Your mom is pretty. Your dad looks nice."

"Thanks." I am now watching her look at the photo. She's staring hard, like she's getting lost in it. Maybe she's fallen into a bad-family-Christmas-photo-trance, and it's up to me to rescue her.

"So, do you want something to eat?" I say, attempting to break the trance.

She shakes her head. "No thanks. Can I see your room?"

I lead her upstairs to my room. My clothes are all over the floor, damn me, Sally, a sea of black cotton. She doesn't seem to notice—she examines the movie posters on my wall, the bookshelves with all of my journals, the school stuff all over my desk.

"Wow, you have one of those word processors," she says, running her hands over the gray plastic.

"Yeah, my dad got that for me when I graduated eighth."

"He seems nice."

You already said that, Leslie Gray Martin, I want to say, but instead I swiftly kick myself under the table and keep my mouth shut.

She continues to look around in silence, and I have to wonder, what now? Do we put make-up on each other and brush each other's hair? Do we have a tickle fight? Do we experiment with homosexuality?

She sits down on my bed with her hands under her thighs.

"I like your room. It's comforting."

I feel like all the forward momentum, the whole thrust of the day has now come to an abrupt stop and is just sitting there, idling. But I can't say why.

"It's not that cool," I say, leaning against my desk, trying to look casual. "I'll bet you have an awesome room."

She looks at me, and her eyes, normally diamond-crusted clouds of blue, flatten out to a dull gray. Her skin no longer seems like translucent sparkly gloss but is now a matte yellow.

"Yeah, it's okay. It gets old though, like everything else. School. Friends. You know?"

I nod, not really understanding. I can't stop staring at her hands. Her hands under her legs seem wrong. As if Leslie Gray Martin has shrunk or her hands have been cut off.

"I'll bet your room is the coolest," I say, trying to redirect the conversation.

She sighs, looking past me. "Oh yeah. The coolest. Pictures of me everywhere. Me and my friends. Me and my boyfriends. Me in my tiaras and boas and homecoming dresses covering every inch of my wall. It's a museum of me."

And I have to close my eyes, to imagine that, the Leslie Gray Martin Museum. The dazzling exhibit of a spectacular life, the relics of being popular and beautiful and immortal behind glass cases and roped-off corners.

"It's all a waste," she says.

I open my eyes. There it is, that idling sound again, like a car with a bad engine. With lots of exhaust. I don't like exhaust. I don't like fumes. Leslie Gray Martin now seems to smell vaguely of gasoline. I suddenly want to light her on fire.

"No it's not. Your life is perfect. It's amazing. It's an inspiration." I've determined the situation is dire—believe me this situation is dire—if I'm laying this out now, for Leslie Gray Martin, in this kind of bold language. As if just now I've found my voice, and I must give that voice to Leslie Gray Martin.

She blinks at me. Then she starts laughing.

"You're funny, Sally. If only you knew that it's not true. You've just bought into the lie."

And then she stops laughing, and her eyes go from gray to black, like the clothes on my floor, and I just want to shut her up because this is not the Leslie Gray Martin who is going to save me, this is not the one who is going to save us all, this is not the one, this is not the one.

Leslie Gray Martin and I are out of balance now, and it's up to me to fix it, even though my therapist says that living in moderation means not fixating on what I think needs to be fixed. But I turn to my desk with the word processor on it, and I think: *I will give it to her.* That will fix this; it seems like she wants it. It's a moderate gift. But suddenly *moderate* doesn't seem enough to turn this around. I need an extreme thing to balance the not-extreme thing so I can achieve moderation. And so the next thing that happens, in a manner in which the action is faster than the thought that processes it, is that I take a pair of scissors from my desk and approach her, quickly but calmly, with the scissors hidden against my palm, and then before she knows what's happening, I grab a handful of her beautiful bouncy curls and promptly slice it off in one clean slicing motion while she shrieks and pushes me away with two hard, flat palms, so that I stumble backwards on the floor, skidding up against the bottom of my desk chair, and she rises, like a giant, her eyes shocked and wild, frantically feeling for the missing clump, which is now in my hand, which I have safely retrieved from the fake Leslie Gray Martin.

"What the fuck!" she screams, in a hard voice, a voice that cracks open each of my cells and fills them with what had just been taken out. "You bitch!"

And I bring the hair to my nose, and it smells like lavender and brownies and popularity, as she stands overs me collecting herself into a cold resolve, giving me that complex, unknowable look, and I'm smiling now, because there you are, Leslie Gray Martin, there you are, it smells like you, and all is right in the world again.

Everything Cake

Sometimes when he was standing at the copier, James had an odd glimpse of his own amazing younger self. Something about the hidden illumination of the photoconductor reminded him of a teenaged James Nolan, young and handsome, the one no longer visible. These days, there was only what should have been amazing but was not, more candles on the cake but less hair, a well-paying job that was insufferably dull—all a kind of plastic lid over a life that was once an excited gasp but now a stifled sigh.

Tammy, the file clerk in his accounting office, materialized in the copy room every time he was making copies, her own copying duties perfectly timed with his. She was pretty, he thought, if a little chatty. She shuffled about in unfashionable, practical shoes, with a certain clerical energy, no underperforming office machine or low printer toner escaping her attention.

He felt the unspoken desire for him to ask her out. At thirty-five, he still hadn't been able to clear himself from the tangled forest of singlehood, and while he wasn't sure he felt too thrilled about Tammy, more and more he'd been harboring the fear that opportunities were limited in number and that any given *No* might be the final nail hammering into his dating life. So because he didn't want a final anything, he asked Tammy to go out with him while the copier was spitting out three copies of his quarterly report, collated.

On Friday, he picked her up at her apartment in his fully loaded Camry financed at three percent interest and took her to his favorite diner. They ordered drinks and read the big menus silently until, five burger descriptions into the prolific burger section, it occurred to him that conversation was uncomfortably missing. The problem was they had already covered a fair amount of ground in the break room. He already knew she had two cats, for example, which were always getting in trouble. Her mother was under the weather these days. She had her eye on a new sedan but was probably going to save the money for a tropical vacation.

The waiter brought out his beer and her white wine. She ordered chicken and dumplings, and he ordered a bacon burger with extra cheese.

"Do you like working at the office?" he finally asked after taking several gulps of beer that nearly emptied the glass, the early sweet taste of a night unwinding.

"I like it a lot," she answered. "The benefits are excellent, don't you think?"

He nodded. She was exactly right; the benefits were excellent. His knee surgery from an old football injury had been completely covered five years earlier. He wondered if he should mention that, but he wasn't sure why, exactly, he would.

"I really want to be an administrative assistant," she said. "If the position opens up, Mr. Jones told me he would hire me."

"You would make a good admin," he commented, trying to be polite.

"Thank you," she said.

"Do you live alone?" she asked him.

He nodded reluctantly. It was true that he was alone when he came home from work, fixed a plate of food, slipped into his room, turned up the music and ate, thinking of nothing. But it was not true that there wasn't someone else in the house while he did all of this. Not true that this someone wasn't his mother.

But there was no need to go into that. Not on a date. If this was even a date. It was the first time in almost two years he'd gone out with a woman his mother hadn't set him up with, but before that he recalled a dating life that had been more vivid and revolving. Less formalities, more alcohol. It's not that there was anything categorically wrong with Tammy. She seemed pleasant enough. But this whole thing felt like an extended conversation in the copy room, just with fancier clothes.

"What kind of music do you like?" he asked, a small bead of sweat threatening to break at his forehead.

"Um, all kinds, I guess," she said, shrugging, before taking a sip of her wine, then her water—to ensure moderation, James assumed—and didn't say anything further. It seemed it was up to him to somehow erase, recant, or genetically alter this conversation into better dialogue.

"I only ask because I thought maybe sometime we could go to a concert," he riffed. She perked up at this.

"Which band did you have in mind?"

He frowned, officially stumped. He had no band in mind.

"I don't know. We could check out who's coming to town."

She shrugged and nodded, which he decided was a draw. The waitress brought out salads, and they fell into another silence, chewing on their veggies and lettuce.

He looked out the window at the cars on 206. An expectation lingered, the unspoken demand for him to carry the conversation valiantly on his shoulders. But work seemed to be their only subject of discussion.

"Do you notice how there are never any men file clerks?" he said, his eyes still on the window.

"What do you mean?"

He looked at her. "Men are never file clerks. Or secretaries."

"I don't think that's true."

"It's mostly true. If not totally."

Tammy paused, a forked tomato in hand. "So what's your point?"

"I don't know. I don't know what my point is."

She looked away. He was saying the wrong things, probably, but he couldn't stop it. He was headed down an icy mountain on oiled skis.

"I mean, did you ever think about being more than an admin to an accountant?" he said.

"More, as in what?"

"Like an actual accountant? I mean—is there a reason you want to aim so low? You seem smart."

She popped the tomato off her fork, back into the salad. "I am smart. And I don't think being an admin is aiming low. It's a perfectly respectable job."

He nodded and didn't say anything.

She dropped the fork into the salad and crossed her arms. "I don't understand what you're saying."

"I just mean, maybe you're selling yourself short. Maybe that's the problem."

"What problem, exactly, are you talking about?"

He scratched his head. How had they ended up in backwards replay, with her tomato and fork back in the salad? He didn't know the problem, but that wasn't the point. The point was that he was just talking about setting one's sights higher. Certainly that was not as awful as her face was suggesting. He searched for a safe, neutral subject. Her cats. Her mother.

Tammy tapped one finger against her arm. The waiter brought out her chicken and his burger, piled high with bacon. A pile he wanted to shove his face in and go to bacon town, the way he could when he was younger and not get soft in the middle.

"I'd like to know, James. What, exactly, is *the problem?*"

He stared at her. The smell of the bacon was torturing him.

She looked away and shook her head, mouthing something to herself.

This is bad, he thought. Now she was staring out the window, thinking. If he had to guess, probably wishing for his swift death.

"You were right about the benefits," he said. "I had knee surgery a few years back from a football injury. I played football in high school. Did you know that? I was a quarterback. I was in really good shape back then. I mean, really good. I was an athlete, but kinda edgy too. Like a cool athlete. I got a tattoo in high school. No one else was doing that then. Do you have any tattoos? Mine's tribal."

She looked back at him and blinked a few times. Less angry, more surprised. A positive emotional shift, he decided.

"Are you dense?" she asked.

"No," he said, but he shrugged, as if unsure.

Then Tammy signaled the waitress over and asked for the check, split.

James' townhouse was a two-story, two-bedroom, two-and-a-half bath with a fenced-in backyard and a porch. The home had been new construction in a brand new development that advertised, "Why buy someone else's dream when you can build your own?" He got to select his counters and cabinets and paint, a dream made of Formica and pine and vintage brown. But when it was done it seemed less than grand. New but cheap. He tried to make up for it by buying a huge wraparound leather couch, full-priced at Macy's, a 52" flat-screen TV—the biggest on the market at the time—and some expensive framed art. Minimal, but tasteful. Minimal but with a mother, curved into the shape of the ugly gray recliner she had him haul from her apartment, seated in front of the flat screen, in perpetual awe of plasma technology, which she didn't seem to notice burning out faster than James would have liked.

The townhouse was a strategy to rewire his life from lights-out-at-nine to lights-out-at-dawn. The home was closer to Philly, where he had gone through two interviews at a big accounting firm and was confident he would be offered the job. The South Jersey-side townhouse would shorten his commute into the city but allow him more affordable living, which was sure to maximize his quality of life at a better cost.

But he never got the call from the firm. Instead, he got an offer from a backup firm in his hometown, out of which he had just moved. Then he got the call from his mother, who had given up the lease on her apartment but was wait-listed at a nearby retirement center. After that her air-dried nylons and shower caps and impractically small drinking glasses moved into his house, where it had all been sitting around in domicile limbo for almost two years.

He spent one night a week with her in front of the TV if only to quell her complaints that he never spent any time with her. Wednesdays, like every night for her, was *Wheel of Fortune* and a TV dinner. *TV Dinner of Fortune*, he referred to it once, silently, finding it to be quite clever on his part. She loved to try to solve the puzzles right out of the chute, before any letters had been turned.

"Jumping to conclusions!" she shouted out, after Pat Sajak had announced a new puzzle.

"The puzzle is a quotation, Mom," James said, as he munched on his spaghetti-with meatballs-for-one.

"*Jumping to conclusions* is a quotation," she said, excitedly.

"No it's not."

"Then what is it?"

He tried to think. "I don't know, but it's not a quotation."

Vanna White turned an *S* around.

"Living on easy street!" she shouted. "I know that's it!"

"Can you read?" James scowled. "There are six words in the puzzle. That's only four."

She dismissed him with a wave of her hand. The contestant on TV spun the wheel.

James stabbed a meatball, embarrassed that he was arguing with his mother about *Wheel of Fortune*. He shoved the entire meatball, drenched in a sauce made with at least an entire shaker of salt, in his mouth. Ever since his six-pack had disappeared, eating always produced a dull anxiety he could never quite locate. At the same time, he found a guilty pleasure in devouring this preservative-laden food, as recently it was the only thing that seemed to touch the unfillable hole in his life.

At the commercial, his mother cut into her own dinner, Salisbury steak with mashed potatoes and a brownie, as if she was refueling for the next round. "How was your date last Friday with that woman from your office?" she asked, her mouth full of steak, eyes still glued to the TV.

He had hoped she wouldn't bring it up, but why wouldn't she, the two of them were marooned here, she from senior citizen life and he from normal dating. He had in the past agreed to a couple of dates with her friends' daughters—including a forty-five-year-old divorced Walmart employee and a widow with a disturbingly large seashell collection. Meanwhile, viable women roamed on some other distant shore, warned to stay away from the dry land where a beached seventy-year-old in nylon stockings was too difficult to move.

But the thought of regurgitating the truth about his date with Tammy now seemed akin to actual vomiting. The truth of that evening would be his last shred of privacy. Losing that meant she would have extracted everything from him, including his manhood, possibly even his humanity.

"It was amazing," he lied. "We're going on a second date."

"How wonderful!" she said, turning to him now with a huge grin that was arguably as vomit-inducing. "How do you two get along?"

What a ridiculous question, he thought. Redundant, considering he'd told her there was a second date, and meaningless, anyway. He wasn't sure how anyone got along let alone how one's getting along related to another person's getting along.

"We get along swimmingly," he said, with a staged smile. He hoped that word, a word from her time, would satisfy her into a fat, content silence, but she squinted at him like she was trying to read something far away.

"What the hell does that mean?" she asked.

He looked at her, wondering if he should just leave the room, silently declaring a forfeit. But it seemed important that she know he was in charge of his own life.

"It means I'm going on another date with her. Not this weekend but the next."

"Oh!" she said, in a happy squeak. "That's fantastic."

He nodded, not looking at her, then stood and walked into the kitchen. But he paused at the counter, the empty tray in his hand. *TV Dinner of Fortune*, he repeated silently, but it was not so funny now. His life seemed exactly the kind of prize one might win at *TV Dinner of Fortune*. A thousand milligrams of sodium and a mother who wouldn't move out.

His life used to be something. Something else. In high school he'd had lots of friends, but after graduation he found his number of friends dwindling as they married off. They all seemed to have fallen into the same pit, face first—that adult grave where fun and youth were buried alive under marriage and mortgages and babies. But at least it wasn't a grave with a mother in it.

A quick thought of his mother in a grave appeared, straightening his spine. How could he think such an awful murderous thing, even if briefly? Did that make him an awful, murderous thinker?

He dumped his TV dinner in the trash and went upstairs to bed.

TAMMY'S copying needs no longer converged with James's. He made copies alone to the lonely, droning whir of the copier. Sometimes he lingered in the room even after the collation was complete, hoping she might appear. Maybe he could set things right so that by the time the weekend rolled around the second date would have turned from a lie into the truth.

He found her on Friday afternoon in the copy room during the lunch hour, when he usually snuck off to a restaurant a little farther out of town for a whiskey lunch. She was at the far end of the room stapling packets of paper, her back to him.

"Hi, Tammy," he said.

"Hi," she said quickly, not turning around. She stapled her packets in an assertive, methodic rhythm.

"Any big plans for the weekend?"

She nodded. "Yep."

Asking her what plans, exactly, seemed apt to make him feel even more left out. What else was there to say? He glanced at a corkboard on the wall that advertised various important notices. A birthday flyer for Gary, one of the junior accountants, had recently been pinned to the board.

"Are you going to Gary's birthday party next month? Everyone in the office is invited."

"Probably," she said. He stared at her back, waiting for her to turn around. But she just stapled.

He had a sudden sense that the planets were severely misaligned. This would have never happened in high school. Girls lined up around the lockers for any scrap of attention from him. Girls were also less complex back then, less easily offended. More contented by football trophies and six-packs. A good joke every once in a while was plenty of talk. Now it was all about conversation and chivalry, what you were and weren't saying, what you could and couldn't do, the subtext of the subtext.

Back then it had been so easy, so unchanging. But maybe that was the problem. Things changed. But when? And why? Could anyone tell him why he was getting a cold back instead of a face, bright and open and inviting?

He felt tired all over. He turned and left. Packed up his things and went home, sending an email to his boss about taking a half sick day.

Friday was grocery day, which meant that his mother was out on her only excursion for the week. He rooted around in the fridge that had been commandeered by her, by way of Jell-O molds and homemade cranberry sauce. His mother, a woman in his life, but the wrong woman.

He pulled a covered dish from the back of the fridge and placed it on the counter, removing the tinfoil. He was surprised to discover a cake his mother used to make him when he was younger. It was called an Everything Cake, and it had all of his favorite things: strawberries, nuts, peanut butter chips, jelly beans—even gum. The frosting was made with all four colors in the food coloring box because he could never choose. "Because my boy can have everything he wants," she would say.

He examined the cake, a hacked version of a baked good. It looked horrible with its bits of candy and nuts and strawberries stuck everywhere. She hadn't made this in years, and he had no idea why now. He wasn't even sure that those things were his favorite things anymore.

He pulled a fork from the drawer and made a vertical slice down the edge. It took a bit of force to drag it through the dense filling.

He brought the bite to his mouth. The flavors made up combinations unholy in nature. Peanut butter and a Sweet Tart, nuts and a jellybean. But as he took another bite, an old sensation returned, that of being a kid and the pleasure of eating everything he loved all at once.

He thought of his father, a brute of a guy. A guy who liked to drink beer and watch sports, loved to fish. He had played football in high school as well—when James was in grade school he would pull the trophies out of the attic and line them up along his bed, pretending that they were being presented to him—State Champions '67, State Champions '68, MVP '68. His dad had married the prom queen, which had been his mother, verified in the pictures she used to keep around the house when his father was alive, a foxy blonde standing next to his dad, as if she had been a different person with his father, a better, more exotic person. The kind of power his father possessed.

Even his death by drowning, after his boat capsized on a fishing trip in Maine, seemed powerful in its own way. Especially with the reports that he was trying to save another man who was drowning.

James went to take another bite but there was none. The cake was gone. He had eaten the entire cake in some kind of entranced binge. He stared at the empty plate, swirling with a sugar high that made him want to burst out laughing in a way that seemed not quite right. His gut was working up a slow tumble, then it was starting to churn, then it was a washing machine in full swing, with way too much detergent. He ran for the bathroom, holding his mouth.

In a few violent retches, nearly the entire cake came right back up. Every bite now in the toilet. Every small, amazing bite. He flushed the toilet and wiped his mouth, disgusted that he couldn't even keep it all in him.

On Saturday he told his mother he was taking Tammy to a matinee and drove himself to the Cinema 10, where he watched a sappy love story starring two popular actors, who probably led glamorous off-screen lives. The tub of buttery popcorn in his lap coated the acidic feeling that burned in his stomach. Afterward he got a table in the corner of a moderately priced steakhouse and ordered the surf and turf and brownie-a-la-mode for dessert. When he was finished, he drank double whiskey and sodas, watching couples and families and friends rotate in and out. He was still hungry and bored and in a foul mood. When the waitress cut him off at five whiskey and sodas he went home, thankful his mother was asleep.

The imaginary dates with Tammy continued. He described these dates in great detail to his mother, who actually turned Pat Sajak down to listen. James and Tammy went to the zoo, where they saw flamingos and snapping turtles, and she pet a gorilla for the first time. The next Saturday at the opera, Tammy fell asleep and later confessed she hated opera but was too polite to say, which gave them both a good laugh over pie at the diner. The following weekend, he surprised her by taking her on a shopping spree at the mall where he let her pick out a dress, a necklace, and shoes—red strappy ones with a stiletto heel—for a surprise date he had planned for the following Saturday. The surprise date was the romantic coup d'état—a drive into New York City for a walk in Central Park, then dinner and a Broadway show. On that Saturday he actually did drive into the city, not New York but Philadelphia, and walked around for a long time, looking at the expensive brownstones. Then he sat outside of the accounting firm that didn't give him a job, ate fast food out of the bag, and imagined a life busting at the seams with dates, a life where he could fit into thirty-four-inch pants again.

"When will I meet her?" his mother asked, over her cardboard meatloaf, cornbread, and mashed potatoes.

James piled chicken teriyaki and noodles into his mouth. He should have known this was coming. He did, in fact, know this was coming, in a sense, but that sense was drowning in the steady stream of food he had practically been mainlining over the past two months. His waist had gone up another pant size, and he was having more trouble identifying where his chin started.

"Look," he said, pointing to the TV. "They're about to solve the puzzle."

"A mother should meet the woman in her son's life."

"I don't think that's the answer to the puzzle," he said, laughing, hoping it would distract her, and she would forget about everything.

She didn't say anything. He could feel her eyes on him. "Are you embarrassed to bring her home?"

He crammed the last of the noodles into his mouth, disappointed it was his last bite. Was it just him or were these TV dinners getting smaller? He could have eaten at least three more.

"James," she said, a little louder.

"What?" he asked, turning toward her, swallowing his salty carbs.

"If your father were here, you'd bring her around. You're embarrassed by me."

He sighed. "If Dad were here, you wouldn't be here." He threw his fork in his tray, feeling sullen and hungry. "In fact, everything would be different. You'd actually have a life instead of sponging off of mine."

"If you want me to leave, you could just say," she said, putting her fork down into her half-eaten tray of food.

No he couldn't, he thought, his eyes on the TV, where the wheel was spinning toward Bankrupt. He couldn't say. Because what would that make him? The man who threw his mother out of the house. He wanted to be the man who patiently helped his mother get back on her feet.

"I have a life," she continued. "Whether I have a life or not has nothing to do with your father."

"Oh come on," he said looking at her. "He made you a better person. More interesting. More attractive."

She looked at him, her face elongated into a surprised shape. "James," she said. "No one makes you anything. You're responsible for that yourself. Besides, your father was no saint." She pulled her slipping nylons up under her robe.

"You're not supposed to say that, Mom, especially after someone dies."

"Well, he wasn't."

"Oh yeah?" James leaned forward, clasping his hands together. "Tell me why he wasn't a saint."

"Well," she said, sitting back in her chair. "He had a mouth on him, that's for sure. He never thought before he said something. He could cut someone down to zero, just like that."

In James's mind, Tammy's offended look appeared, an unhappy, floating head. "So he was blunt. What's wrong with that?"

"Nothing, if you don't want to have any friends. Your father had no friends at the end of his life. He was too mean. He thought everyone else had it all wrong. That kind of thinking is a lonely grave."

James imagined his father not having any friends. Surely this wasn't true—he was so confident, so likeable.

"He had friends," James argued. "The last thing he did was take a trip up to Maine with some friends to go fishing!"

"He went alone, dear," she said. "He didn't know anyone on that boat."

James frowned, remembering his father talk about fishing with the boys or drinking with his buddies. But he could not attach a face to any of these men. He could picture no buddies. He saw only the three of them—mother, father, James.

"Well, he was a hero at least," he said finally.

"What are you talking about?"

"He tried to save that passenger."

"Where did you get that?"

James started to answer but didn't have one. Where *did* he get that? He had heard that, hadn't he? "Your father couldn't swim. He drowned because he couldn't swim."

James looked at his mother, her arms on the armrest, her re-nyloned feet sticking up on the ottoman, stretched out, permanent. Why couldn't his father have been here instead of her?

"That's ridiculous." James said.

"You're damn right. It's ridiculous that he would go out on a small boat when he couldn't swim. I tried to tell him, but he wouldn't listen."

James felt a deep shame starting in him like a growl. He was embarrassed now for his father, a man who couldn't swim, a man who died alone with no friends.

"You can have your arrogance or you can have friends. But you can't have both," his mother said.

She meant he couldn't have everything. Despite what she had told him as a boy. A boy could have everything. But a man, a man could not. A man couldn't have what he had when he was young. A man couldn't have his father. A man couldn't even have the memory of that father.

Gary's birthday party was on a Saturday night at the country club. James felt it might be his only chance to patch things up with Tammy. Or a chance to meet another girl, one he could actually take home. He might even dance with this new girl he might meet.

The problem was shirts. None of them buttoned over his burgeoning belly. On the way to the party he stopped by the mall and tried on half-a-dozen shirts at the department store, all of which made him look like various versions of a pregnant whale. He finally picked a wide-fit button-down that the bored salesgirl told him looked great too many times for him to actually believe her.

By the time he got to the party he was two hours late, and the place was teeming with people. At least a hundred, James estimated. In his survey of the room, he imagined that this was his own birthday party and that all of these people were here for him. But the vision quickly dissolved to a room with only him and his mother, sliding around on the dance floor, she in her nylons and robe.

He spotted Tammy in a group of dancers. She was wearing a short blue dress, and her hair was piled on top of her head. He waved. She turned away, pretending she didn't see him.

He went over to the buffet table, which appeared to be endless. He had sworn he would eat moderately. Not take everything, like he wanted to. He started at the front of the table, putting a little bit of salad on his plate, some veggies, a small piece of bread. But as he kept walking, the dishes just kept presenting themselves in enticing fashion. By the end of the table his oath had disintegrated under a pound of food on his plate.

He sat down at a table alone and ate. Everyone was dancing or mingling. The thought of dancing, though awful to him at the moment, seemed only plausible after consuming the right amount of alcohol.

He finished his food, which took some time, and sat there, stuffed, wondering if he should talk to some folks. But he felt bloated and sour and really didn't want to entertain any conversation about work. Tammy was now over at the desert bar, selecting cookies for her plate. Had she really pretended not to see him?

Maybe she hadn't seen him. That was a possibility, wasn't it? He stood up and walked over to the desert bar.

"Hi Tammy," he said, standing next to her with his arms down.

She turned toward him. "Hi," she said flatly.

"You look nice."

"Thanks."

"So I was thinking, maybe we could try again at that date."

Her eyes darted nervously past him toward her friends, then back at him. "I'm sorry but I can't."

He felt an immediate dread. His mother would ask him about Tammy and the party tomorrow, and he'd have to concoct a bigger lie. The thought made him feel as if everything he had eaten was coming back up, just like the cake.

"It probably wouldn't work out anyway," he told her.

"Then why did you even ask?" she said.

He sighed and studied her pursed face. She was fully frowning. He recognized this look from years ago; he got the same look every time he dumped a girl. The angrier they looked, the more they wanted him. But now Tammy was just angry, and it had nothing to do with wanting him.

"I'm sorry," he said.

She shook her head and then turned, walking away. He watched her go and thought about how he would break this to his mother. She wasn't going to like this one bit. But it was the only way.

He wandered outside, where there was a pool and an outside bar. It was the beginning of fall and starting to get chilly, so no one was out there except the bartender. He sat at the bar and ordered a double whiskey and soda.

After two more double whiskey and sodas, a woman came out from a side door and sat down next to him. She was in a black warm-up suit, as if she had been jogging.

"Coke with extra ice," she told the bartender. Then she pulled an enormous purse up on the bar and started to dig through it.

"Hell of a party," she said, into her purse.

"Sure," he answered, leaning over his drink.

She produced a pack of cigarettes. "I'm totally kidding. This party sucks."

He watched her pull a cigarette out and light it. She seemed familiar, but he couldn't place her face. Her age was undecipherable—she seemed young in an old way. There were wrinkles around her mouth and eyes that didn't appear to be from age, but from something else. Too many cigarettes, perhaps.

"Do you work at Jones and Doogle?" he asked.

She looked at him, blowing smoke out of the side of her mouth. "I work for the country club. Mostly banquets and parties."

The bartender pushed the Coke toward her.

"Do you work for Jones and Whoever?" she asked. "What is that by the way? Am I looking at bankers or accountants here?"

"Accountants. Good guess."

She shrugged. "I see a lot of these parties. Guys in suits. You learn how to differentiate the nuances in mediocrity. No offense."

He looked down at his shirt. "I'm not wearing a suit," he said.

"Right. Is this your boss's party? You had to come?"

James shook his head. "Co-worker." He pointed through the window at Gary, who was boogying down like a moron on the dance floor with Janet from human resources.

The woman watched Gary for a moment. "Well, I'd be drinking at the bar too if my co-worker was a tool. Of course, I'd be drinking either way. I just can't drink here, where I work. Club rules. Not even really supposed to smoke. But I can't let them take everything, right?"

He watched her suck down most of her Coke with extra ice. Something about her made him feel at ease, like it was impossible to say the wrong thing to her. As if the wrong thing didn't exist. He realized she was pretty, deceptively pretty, in fact. Olive skin and a perfect nose. The cigarette didn't seem to quite fit her.

"I'm James," he said

She smiled and tipped her glass toward him. "Amelia."

Amelia, he repeated silently. *A unique name*, he thought. But somehow one he had heard before. "I knew an Amelia, in high school," he remembered after a moment. He stirred his drink and pictured that Amelia. That Amelia was clean and unwrinkled and would never have become a smoking waitress.

"Oh yeah, which high school?"

"Seneca."

She narrowed her eyes. "What year?"

"Ninety-four."

"James," she said, as if searching a database. "James Nolan. You played football."

"Yes," he said, a flare of excitement going off in him.

"I'm the Amelia," she said. "We were in the same class. Amelia Farrow."

"You're the Amelia," he repeated in a kind of dreamy wonder. This was the Amelia. Except nothing like her, it seemed—class president and yearbook editor. Still, it was someone he knew. And someone who knew him.

"Wow, what are the odds?" she said.

"Um, pretty high actually."

She laughed, which surprised him. He hadn't meant it to be a joke. He seemed to have lost his ability to know what was funny or not. He smiled.

"I never thought you'd be a waitress."

He wanted to say, *I thought you'd shoot higher*, but it dawned on him now that this was the kind of thing that ended dates early for him.

"I never thought you'd be an accountant."

This surprised him. She said that like it was a bad thing, being an accountant. But, really, was it so great? His current job had been a backup offer, one he didn't want, to an offer he didn't get but that if he was really being honest, he hadn't wanted either. When he was younger he'd wanted to be a pilot, an exciting job with some risk, but that dream had wandered away while he wasn't looking, and he'd drifted and settled. He was the one who hadn't shot higher.

Amelia was watching him in a way he couldn't read, like Tammy, like his mother, like all women. What, exactly, is *the problem*? he could hear Tammy saying.

But the more he sat there, looking at Amelia looking at him, the more he thought that maybe it wasn't women who were hard to read, it was himself. If he could understand himself maybe he'd know how to have conversations that didn't end dates early, that didn't result in him pointing out in some other person a problem that just might be exclusively his own.

"I'm sorry," he said. "I didn't mean to say that."

The cigarette was at her lips. She took a drag. "Don't worry about it. Anyway, I didn't think I'd be a waitress either. I used to be a grade school teacher, if you can believe it. I used to be married. Truth is—none of that is better. Better is an illusion. I always say, when you first put your hand in the grab bag, it's exciting because you could come back with anything. Maybe even everything. And then you pull your hand back out, and you realize that it's just any old thing."

He found himself nodding a lot. *I know, I know,* he wanted to say, *go on.* But she was throwing her cigarettes back into her purse. He didn't want her to go. He wanted to keep talking to her.

"Well, gotta go," she said, sliding off her stool and putting her purse over her shoulder. "It was nice to see you, James Nolan. Don't let the bullshit get you down!"

"Thanks," he said, as she flicked her cigarette into the bushes and walked away. He wished he had asked for her number, if only so they could continue the conversation.

James finished his whiskey, ordered another and watched Gary and Janet through the window some more. They were getting hot and heavy. He wondered if Janet would have to file a harassment claim against herself. He checked his watch. It was a quarter to midnight. One more drink, he told himself.

At midnight the lights went on, and some kind of announcement was made over the PA. James wandered back in, a little drunk, thinking he was ready to dance. But everyone came to a stop on the dance floor. James thought of Amelia. Maybe he could call the club tomorrow and ask for her. They could go out. This time he could do it right and not say something about women that maybe, in some way, was really about him. He watched as a caterer rolled the birthday cake out—several large tiers on rollers. It was the biggest cake James had ever seen.

Then the lights went down and a slow, sultry version of "Happy Birthday" came over the PA. Suddenly, something was being pushed up from the top of the cake—a lid of sorts, and a woman was coming out, rising slowly, in a red corset, with a microphone, lip-syncing to "Happy Birthday." The woman was Amelia.

She swayed her hips back and forth as she sang, pointing and curling her finger at Gary, who grinned and ogled Amelia like a drunken animal while taking slaps on the back from the Jones and Doogle employees. Everyone was going wild, hollering and whistling.

James watched Amelia, moving slowly to the music, pretending to sing. She was absolutely stunning. He couldn't believe how beautiful she looked under the twinkling disco ball. He had never imagined that anything so beautiful could come out of a cake. And yet, that meant there was no cake, or not nearly as much as had first appeared, and that made him feel instantly starving, an endless, aching, nested hunger. As if the person he thought he was now was not there, nor was the person he used to be, nor was the person before that, the person he imagined was his father. He watched the dance floor, and Amelia looked at him, and they locked eyes as she lip-synced the words, words not for him because it wasn't his birthday, words she wasn't even singing anyway, and he thought how amazing, how sorrowful, how true, this woman inside the cake.

MARGO GOES DARKO

MARGO GOES DARKO

I have been dragged like something feral and screeching to Open Mic Night at the local Jersey club where a woman on stage is doing animal poetry performance art with a ferret. My boyfriend, Troy, loves this shit, which means theoretically I love it too because theoretically I love him. Truthfully, there is a list of things I would rather be doing, including swimming in acid, receiving experimental shock therapy, scrubbing prison toilets, drowning, or getting a spinal tap. I get through the evening with glasses of vodka. These are free because I'm a person of interest around here. This is a scenario that my seventeen-year-old self would do a backflip over, that of her future twenty-one-year-old self sitting squarely at the center of all the talk around the age difference between her and her boyfriend, whose age does not start with a two, but a three, followed by a four. You do the math. It should be said that my seventeen-year-old self would not have been able to do the math, or any math for that matter, as she was a colossal moron.

Troy is the landscaping poet I met two years ago. He desperately wants to be taken seriously. And I try to, really, because living with him is better than squatting in my Dad's divorced-man apartment. And also because Troy lets me get right next to what I want, which happens to be minimum emotional intimacy. Troy is a person I can be close to at a safe distance instead of far away from at a dangerous one, as is the case with my father.

And now Troy is positioning himself onstage, where he pauses, his head down. I take an enormous swig of vodka. "Heart Rain," he begins, leaning hard into the mic. "The weatherman says it's overcast and dark/Inside is the storm that rages like fire in my heart/The wind of your love rattles the cage of my body/Tears on the window like rain on the glass/ Falling so fast, fast."

Such pitiful near-rhyming is indication that Open Mic is only getting worse. I can't help but think that these unmitigated disasters are my fault. Troy, the ferret lady, and the endless string of hacks before them. These performances seem to prove that the longer I look at something, the more likely it is to perform its worst. Which is why I don't fly, for example. I'm convinced that if I stare long enough out the window at the engines, they will malfunction and rip away from the aircraft, leading to unmitigated engine-induced fatalities. I can't explain the connection between observing a thing and the performance of the thing, but I imagine the problem resides in my mind, which I can't shut down. I can only turn down the noise a little by drinking or committing an act that is numbing and repetitive, like washing my hands twenty to thirty times a day.

My parents are a great example of the effects of my observation. I observed them during all of my childhood, only to watch them break apart like engines from a plane.

After last call, Troy and I return to the house we share with two of his friends from high school, Liam and Ted. It's a too-many-people-for-a-three-bedroom-shithole kind of situation, but Troy keeps telling me we're going to get our own place as soon as he has enough in the bank. Troy says lots of things that aren't true, like he's got an agent interested in his poetry. Also, that we are going to get married. No agent would be interested in Troy's poetry because it is simply atrocious. And also, I'm not going to marry him.

The master bedroom we share is cramped, perpetually dusty, and, as an added bonus, facing the Jersey Turnpike.

The room is not what you would call fit for two adults, but I don't own much except some clothes and a handful of books collected from my part-time gig at the bookstore.

"That was so great tonight," Troy says, sitting on our bed, which is just a mattress, and pulling off his shoes. "That lady with the ferret—at first you're thinking, what is this? And then it just gets inside of you. You know?"

"Something definitely weaseled its way in." I pull off my shirt and bra, slip on one of Troy's T-shirts, and climb into bed with a beer. I am very intoxicated.

"You know, I wish you'd get more involved." His shoes are off now, and he's just sitting with his back to me, a little hunched over. He is very sober.

"What do you mean?"

He turns toward me halfway, steadying himself with one arm. "I just wish you'd get into it more. Instead of just sitting there drinking."

"I don't just sit there drinking."

"Yes, you do. In fact, somehow you're still sitting there drinking."

"What do you want me to do, get up and shit a poem?"

"No. I want you to be more open. If you jump into the river of your heart, don't be surprised if it leads to an ocean."

Troy loves vomit-inducing quotes. So much so it makes me question how long we can actually go on.

"Who said that one?"

"Anonymous."

"Sounds like anonymous needs to jump into the river of alcohol."

Troy pushes off the bed, sighing extra hard, and disappears into the bathroom, slamming the door shut. I hear the water in the sink running.

This has been Troy's routine lately, his not-so-happy-with-Margo routine. First, he sighs a lot, then he slams things around, and then he turns on a faucet as if he's so angry he just needs to do something sink-related. Which I would understand, given my own sink-related habits, but this is all for show. He's most likely leaning against the door, waiting for what seems like enough time before he can turn off the water and return to bed, with more sighing, until I decide I can't stand it anymore and must become snuggly and apologetic.

The water shuts off in the bathroom, and I prepare my prolific apology. To be fair, I have been a little difficult lately. But with my twenty-second birthday in two weeks, I feel that parts of me grew up too quickly, and other parts stopped growing a long time ago, and the result is this grotesquely assembled, deformed adult.

The things that have grown too fast: my cynicism and my sexuality.

The things at a standstill: all that still hurts me.

On Wednesday, Rae, a friend of the roommates, calls to tell me she is getting a tattoo. Rae is in her late twenties and the only other woman in the group. Through some additional fucked up twist of fate, she even graduated from my high school years earlier. All of this apparently means we are best friends, and the onus is on me to accompany her to the tattoo shop.

At the tattoo place she tells an overly inked gentleman devoid of any smiling mechanism that she wants a butterfly with a heart on its wing on her ankle. The butterfly has a special meaning, and the heart on the wing has some other special meaning, but I can't remember either meaning because I was only pretending to listen when she told me. I find it's hard to listen to a person when you have no interest in what that person is saying.

She sits in the chair while he sets up his station. When he tests his needle, she makes a wincing face, like she's already in pain. I can't imagine why anyone would put themselves through this for some picture that, while permanent, is still destined to fade.

"So I'm thinking a dinner party at my house for your birthday," she says between winces. "What do you think?"

Rae's whole thing is dinner parties. I know this because she's always dragging me to movies that have these kinds of parties in them. What she wants is culturally diverse, upwardly mobile, stylish adults who assemble to drink and talk philosophy on a weekly basis in some modern-architected home. In this group there would be at least two homosexuals, a published author, and a British person. Also, a handsome single man in a fashionable blazer, looking for love. What Rae gets, instead, is five un-sophisticates, more or less, talking the same old banal shit around a collapsible kitchen table in her apartment. Rae is not as bad as the guys; it seems like she's trying very hard to transition into serious adulthood but she's a little behind the ball, and the transition is taking an abnormally long time. Plus, she lives in this apartment that's over-furnished with do-it-yourself things like homemade curtains and decorative objects she made from a how-to book. The whole vibe reminds me of the house I share with Troy, which gives me the general sense that I'm headed for something dull and terrible and backward. Had I known this was ahead, I would have told that seventeen-year-old Margo to *Turn back, turn back! Road impassable.*

But Rae is trying to be nice to me. So I shrug. "A dinner party sounds fine."

"You're funny," she says. "You're monumentally under-whelmed. I was like that too when I was younger, believe it or not."

I do not believe it. In no way do I think that Rae was ever underwhelmed about anything. She's all *sunny side up* and I'm all *scourge the earth*, which is what made me kind of despise her at first. Yet somehow, while I was running over her with my rampant cynicism I inadvertently managed to win her over. Call it the mysterious magnetism of youth. Now she finds me funny and odd, like an object in a museum, one that she wants to look at again and again.

The needle buzzes. I remember how much I wanted a tattoo in high school because I stupidly believed it would bond me to James Nolan, the hot senior with some tribal thing inked on his arm. That was the year before my parents split. The tattoo artist hits Rae's ankle and begins outlining in black, drawing the wings of the butterfly. I tune out her occasional shrieks and concentrate on that needle. Its brassy drilling sound creates a constant hum that reminds me of my mother, who always hummed a soft song while doing dishes. That hum was the only sound of comfort I had since my parents had stopped speaking to each other. Our lives had become a silent performance—forks into mouths, glasses against lips, napkins to hands. An existence strung together by gestures and pantomimes. This charade went on for almost a year. It became normal. It became my parents. They were a strange and silent ship that sailed in and out of the harbors of my days. Until they announced they were divorcing and I looked—I really looked at that ship—and discovered they weren't on it. It was just an empty ship, sailing around and around. A ghost ship. And there wasn't love. And that wasn't-ness filled me with something that was. A worry that kept multiplying. An infestation of worries so big that I had to make certain places dead, places I had to put a fist to over and over. Inside, I was a this-and-that of terror and nothing, terror and nothing.

The tattoo artist outlines the heart. With no color it's just an empty heart, a trace heart, the shape of something that should be there, but is not.

On Saturday afternoon Troy works on poetry, and I work on listlessly flipping through channels, landing on a show called *Buddy the Guppy*, the latest craze in kid TV. Something burns inside of me, my pending birthday, the fact that *Buddy the*

Guppy doesn't actually rhyme, all that seems out of place and not-quite-right about adulthood.

Liam and Ted play chess at the table. They mutually suck at chess, among other things. I often forget they are not actually brothers, two stocky men who both have red hair and dull eyes. Decades together seems to have morphed them into the same being. They co-own one of those hobby shops and are into tiny replicas of the real thing in any and all variety. This includes girlfriends—Liam has a penchant for giggly Asian women, and Ted doesn't appear to date anyone over twenty-five. He was dating a nineteen-year-old when I met him, but considering the implications of my own age-gapped relationship, I am forced to relegate him to that area of my mind where I can reasonably make a case that he's simply an idiot who is incapable of mature, adult relationships as opposed to a pedophiliac predator.

"What's the best advice you ever received?" Troy asks me, pen paused above his notebook.

Troy likes to ask questions that appear to engage others in stimulating conversation, but this, too, is a show. He doesn't care about the answer, just the question itself, and asking it. It's what the asking will do for him, a false interrogation, a false love. He was married once in his early twenties and sometimes I picture a blow-up doll bride, one that he could talk at without interruption. I suppose, in the aimless wander since his divorce, he has sensed that there is a cosmic emptiness within him, and so he asks questions in search of answers he thinks will fill it. What he doesn't realize is that these questions come from an empty place and are in fact empty themselves.

"Don't get pregnant," I say.

He sticks his chin up and frowns into the air.

"I was seventeen. It was really great advice."

"That's funny," he says, but he's not laughing.

"I've gotten a lot of great advice," he says after a moment. "I particularly love: Reach for the moon...if you miss at least you'll be among the stars."

This feels like another gem by Anonymous. Other gems have included: "My love for you is a journey. Starting at forever and ending at never." (Spoken to me on our fourth date.) Also: "If you hear an onion ring, answer it." (Troy's idea of a joke.) Troy would be able to get away with these gems if I didn't read so much and hadn't discovered that there were just some things that should never, in the history of man, have ever been penned. Troy's poetry, for example.

He's writing in his notebook now, probably other good advice. He will most likely spin all of this into his new poem called "Advice." "Don't get pregnant." It would begin. "Burn fat, not bridges. Don't look a gift horse in the mouth or in any other orifice for that matter. It's a bad idea to marry that guy who roofied you."

"Are you coming with me to the club tomorrow night? It's another chance for you to have an open mind."

"I have to work," I say, realizing that Buddy the Guppy has asked some question and is waiting for the viewers to answer. The awkward pause makes me itch, internally. In fact, I'm crawling out of my skin. It makes me want to wash my hands.

Troy is sighing, loud. Good thing for both of us there's not a sink nearby.

It's also a good thing for both of us that Troy doesn't know that sometimes I tell him I'm working, but instead I go to bars and talk to men. Not sexy or dirty talk, necessarily. Just perfectly normal, everyday talk.

It's nice to meet you. Tell me about your day.

Does that turn you on?

No. I just want to hear what you did today.

I don't understand.

Just tell me about your day. Just lay it out for me.

OK. I went to work and had lunch with a colleague. In the afternoon I ran some errands.

What kind of errands?

Oil change, dry cleaners, bank, that sort of thing.

How much was the oil change?

Excuse me?

How much was the oil change?

Thirty bucks.

Not bad. Now tell me about what you dropped off at the dry cleaners.

What happens after is sex, but it's not about sex. That is separate, something I gave away when I was seventeen, after I moved away to a new school. After you give it away, it becomes undebatable, moot. It becomes what you must do, an unavoidable conversation between your body and someone else's. It's just the cleaning-up, the cleansing of the hands. There in the cleansing I think of my mother, whose disappearance I discovered after my parents got divorced, and I rode a bus for two hours only to find all of her clothes removed from the house. I think of my mother's absence from that house as men disappear into the silent empty space that is me.

I COME home the next night, Open Mic Monday, after sleeping with a mechanic, a guy in his late thirties who used to be a football player but is now getting soft, a fact which scares him, especially now that he is separated from his wife. I step into the shower and massage the smell of oil and brake fluid and tune-ups from my hair—but slowly, because I like how the odors are working-class and domestic. The mechanic has a dog and a second mortgage; financial struggles have been the main strain on his marriage. He plays fantasy football, and his sister just had a kid. His car is in the shop, ironically enough. I rinse the shampoo from my hair, lather up soap on my legs and arms and stomach and rinse. My face goes into the water last, because I want to leave all that we have discussed on my lips and in my ears for as long as I can.

When I step out of the shower, Troy is standing there with his arms folded.

I did not expect Troy to be standing there with his arms folded.

"Where were you?" he asks, his head tilted.

"Work," I say, toweling off my hair. I am only mildly panicked, which surprises me. But I don't know if that's because the panic is mild or there at all.

"The thing is," he continues, now tilting his head the other way. "I stopped by the bookstore, and they said you weren't working tonight."

I bring the towel down and hold it in front of me. The last trace of the mechanic is now in my hands.

"I didn't work tonight. I went to a bar and I talked to a guy."

"Which guy?"

"A random guy."

The skin around Troy's eyes wrinkles, and his mouth turns downward.

"We talked. Nothing intellectual or poetic," I go on. "Just plain old talk."

I'm in a place I've never been before, a place where Troy could possibly hear me if he listened closely.

"Did you have sex with him?"

His mouth is now tight, stern; his eyes look past mine. He's not listening to me. This was the way my parents looked at each other, each trapped in their own dark towers, looking out at the nothing on the other side.

"No," I say. This is a lie, and it isn't. Because the question he's asking me is not, *Why do you do such a thing? What are you looking for? Do you hurt?* He wants to know, instead, if I made a fool of him, if I gave away something that belongs to him only, and the answer is I did not. Troy makes a fool of himself, there is nothing of me that belongs to him.

And the thing I want, the thing I want most in the whole world, is for him to say, *Talk to me, Margo. Tell me.*

His face is a mix of anger and confusion. "I don't appreciate the lying. Even if you are just chatting up random men at the bar. I'm going to expect this won't happen again."

He leaves the room. I'm left alone and unheard in the place where there is nothing but me and dead air.

On the last Thursday of every month I have dinner with my dad, who lives a couple of towns over. Troy lets me borrow his car to make the forty-minute drive. When I arrive, Dad's wearing the faded oxford button-down that has two holes in the sleeves, one of the three shirts in his closet on rotation. His beard is unevenly trimmed, which means he did it himself in the bathroom, probably just before I arrived. He is forty-five years old. On a good day he looks sixty.

I usually pick him up and drive him over to a Chinese place for dinner. I make it a habit to spend as little time as possible at his place. All the furniture from our house is in that apartment. It was retrieved after my mom disappeared. It's like our house, only a replica. Our near-house.

"How's work?" I ask him at dinner. It's neutral conversation. I don't care to hear the real answer, and he doesn't care to give it.

"Still paying me." He leans over his plate and shovels lo mein into his mouth.

I take a few big swigs of my beer. This is the first of many drinks I will order before the fortune cookies arrive on a plate.

I talk about the bookstore, which is mostly made up news—like I'm working all the time, I'll probably get promoted, I started a book club that's all the rage now. I don't see this as lying. If I didn't say those things there would be nothing but all we aren't saying, and that feels like an even bigger lie. I talk about Troy as I usually do, vaguely: he's still around, he's still landscaping. But this time it feels even more vague, like he's an object in the distance I'm trying to describe but I have no idea if it's a man or a tree or a mailbox.

I order another beer. Then another. Our plates are cleared. I'm still talking about stuff—my books, the weather, who knows. That burning feeling that usually eats through my stomach has ceased. Dad is quiet, but he doesn't seem disinterested. I talk more. I drink another beer. Dad listens. I haven't talked to him this much, ever. This could be something good, maybe even something great.

Except I'm talking about the mechanic. And the investment banker from three weeks ago. And the PE teacher from last month. Their doctor's appointments, their Roth IRAs, their newly painted crown molding.

I stop talking and try to count how many beers I've had. Five? Six?

"Does Troy know about these men?"

I'm not sure what I've said exactly. Had I told him that I slept with them? Did I mention all of them from this past year?

"Yes and no."

He scratches the back of his head and leans forward in his seat. "These men . . ."

He trails off, looking away. But the trailing-off sparks an old feeling. Like being overturned on a path, dumped off to the side and abandoned. I feel a sudden rage, an urge to flip the table over.

"What?"

He looks back at me, blank.

"*These men* what? Finish your thought."

"I'm not here to interfere."

That is exactly why I'm living this way, I want to say. Hurting and uninterrupted. But I have to say it silently because that's the way that he has taught me to say it.

I drive him home, drunk and swerving. We pull into the parking lot and sit quietly.

"I need coffee before I head home," I say to the windshield.

He makes coffee in the kitchen while I find myself wandering around the living room, running my hand over the brown plaid couch I picked out with my mother. The glass coffee table I once fell and chipped my tooth on. The lamps that don't match each other. I want to gut the place by fire.

I drift into the doorway of the kitchen. Mom's spice rack sits on the counter next to a pie dish that she bought at an antique shop we went to once forever ago. My mother is here, and yet she is not.

"Do you know where she is?" I ask my dad, his back to me. I did not know I was going to ask this.

He finishes pouring the water into the coffee pot and turns around to face me, his eyes gray and unmoving. But I can see a darkening in his pupil, like a cloud forming. This is the way I have learned to know when my father is reacting.

"No," he says quietly.

"Well, have you looked? Because I'd like to know. I mean, I think I deserve to know where she is."

"She doesn't want to be found, Margo."

I cross my arms and plant myself squarely in the doorway. "I don't care what she wants. I want to find her."

"It's better that you don't."

"Why?"

"Because there are things better left as they are."

"Really? My mother disappears, and that's better?"

The coffee starts percolating. Dad leans against the counter, hands in pockets.

"Maybe not for you, no, but for me."

I almost respond but don't. It occurs to me that maybe he never wanted this divorce, that perhaps it was not as mutual as I had been led to believe.

"I know it hurts you, but she is still my mother."

He looks at me and draws in a breath, his eyes narrowing. I know that look. I know that look because I've never seen it. He's about to tell me something.

"We're still married," he says.

We stand there for a long time. So long the coffee finishes percolating.

"What the hell are you talking about?" I say finally.

"We never got divorced."

"What do you mean, you never got divorced? You guys split up, and I moved in with you because you were divorcing. Because you got divorced."

"We started the process, but never finished it. She left before we signed the paperwork."

"So? You couldn't finish it without her?"

"Not without looking for her and not finding her and then filing it with the court. It's a whole other thing that way. So I just let her go."

There were words, there were these words. So many words to come out of my father's mouth at once. I would have been stunned, overjoyed, if they hadn't been so many of the wrong words.

My parents, only nearly divorced, like a near rhyme.

I WAKE up on my birthday after spending two days in bed. I am now twenty-two, and I have to go to a dinner party in honor of this fact.

Liam and Ted bring dates. Liam's, of course, is a Chinese woman who came into his shop. Ted has scrounged up some senior from the local community college. I forget both of their names immediately.

Rae has made some kind of sliced beef with veggies and bread and salad. There is wine. She has put linen out on the table, some fresh flowers. I spot an upside-down pineapple cake in the kitchen. It's all very nice; she's trying hard to make it all very nice.

But there is something in me that does not feel nice. A not-niceness that is unstable and explosive.

"I just think parenting should be more of a peer relationship between kids and adults, you know?" Troy is saying. I don't know how we arrived at this subject. I've been concentrating on the arm he has thrown up on the back of my chair. On how much I want to gnaw on it until it falls off his body.

"There is too much hierarchy," he continues. "Too much discipline. What if we just removed the power struggle? What if we just let our kids do what they want to do?"

"We'd end up with more murderers and pedophiles," I say, catching Ted's eye. There is laughter. He looks away.

"That's the thing," Troy says. "I think parents force kids to break rules by setting them, by getting too involved with them, by over-steering."

"I can't wait to have kids," the college student weighs in.

"Whoa," Ted throws his hands up. "We haven't even had dessert yet."

There is more laughter. I think about the fact that there are no presents. Adult birthday parties never have presents, I've noticed. Everything in the adult world seems false, reversed, like a tiny replica of the real thing.

"I just want a date," Rae says. "When I was twenty they were lining up."

"Looks like Ted is free after dessert," Liam says. Everyone but the college student laughs.

I close my eyes. There is too much laughter and not enough presents. The problem is me, I tell myself. I just need to stop observing. If I stop observing these people, they will start performing better. They will stop making so much noise.

But the conversation rattles on and on and on. In my mind, the room goes from dim to dark. I'm in a cave with cave people I can't see, all talking in surround sound. It's the same incoherent babble in the same tone, at the same decibel level. Never rising and never falling.

I want to take back everything I told myself I came here for, if I can even remember what that was. I want the silence back, the one that was bred into me. I want to lock myself in the closet with my dark fears. I want a strange man holding his hand over my mouth while he pushes his emptiness into me.

A voice from somewhere else presses up against the lid of noise that's trapped me here. "Will you all," it begins, the voice that is not mine but still speaking up through me, shouting through me, actually, "please shut the fuck up."

I open my eyes, and here I am at the table I've now silenced. Troy withdraws his arm from my chair. Every eye is on me.

"What?" Rae asks.

"You're all insufferable dimwits, that's what."

"What's wrong with you?" Rae continues.

"All of your bullshit is what's wrong with me. You people don't know anything. Which isn't even what bothers me. It's perfectly fine not to know anything. It just that you don't know that you don't know anything. And that's the problem. That right there is the problem."

"We do know that we don't know anything," Liam says and then goes silent.

"Yeah," Ted chimes in. "I mean, we're just talking,"

"Exactly," I say. "You're just talking. That's all you ever do. Just talk. There's no meaning in what you say. No beauty. No symmetry. You're all a bunch of near-rhymers."

"Margo . . ." Troy reaches for me but I smack his hand away.

"Don't. Touch me. I have wasted two years of my life listening to your worn out sayings and atrocious poetry. Your poetry is a crime against humanity. It's literary genocide. It's so cloying I want to vomit. Cloy Troy. Ha! Cloy Troy. Now that's a rhyme!"

It appears I've pushed my chair back, away from the table, as if I'm about to make a run for it.

Rae crosses her arms. She looks oddly calm. "I thought you were our friend."

"You did?" I say. "As in your best friend? Best friends forever? Is that why you insisted on throwing me a party and dragging me along with you to get that tattoo? Which by the way is so cliché. Cliché Rae."

She looks at me, her eyes turning into watery circles. The rest of the table appears to be shell shocked. My eyes sweep the group, glossing over the expendable dates, landing on the red-headed wonder twins. Ted avoids my eyes. "And you, dating a sixteen-year-old. I mean, I was young when I met Troy, but she's criminal. Your whole person just oozes male repulsion." I pause. Searching. "Ted the Ped, that's you."

This is getting weird. Beyond weird. I can feel it in my bones. In the bones of a body that has been supporting a heart I can't feel beating, in the skeleton of my hands that have been scrubbed raw under the faucet, hoping they will disintegrate into dust.

Washing my hands sounds like a good idea. I push out of my chair and make for the bathroom. I can hear the chatter return behind me, the flailing nimrods trying to semantically untangle what just happened. I shut and lock the bathroom door. Turn on the faucet and plunge my hands under the water.

I scrub and rinse, scrub and rinse, searching for symmetry and repetition, the back and forth, a pattern to keep out the noise. But it's not there. It's just not there.

Rae's organic grainy soap splits open a sore on my knuckle. I scrub into that sore until it's bleeding, until blood is all over the sink. I turn off the water and wipe my bloody hands on her mismatched towels.

Rae's homemade curtains hang from the window. I want to undo the do-it-yourself, to take apart the grafted-together apartment. I want it to match the inside of me that burns.

I grab a lit candle from the sink and hold it to the edge of the curtains. The flame spreads out across the bottom, consuming the fabric remnant as it climbs up to the curtain rod.

I bound out of the bathroom. Troy is standing up now, pacing. Rae's watery eyes have been dried up by her resumed anger. Liam and Ted pat their girlfriends nervously. The group looks generally wounded.

"You," I point to each person, "are a disease of the mind."

I am a nuclear power plant that has exploded and rained acid on everyone. Troy looks the worst, his face red and pinched, this rare display of silence indicating his stunned embarrassment.

"Do you smell that?" Rae asks, sniffing. "Is that smoke?"

She rises and heads toward the bathroom, where she disappears. What comes next is a shriek. "The wall is on fire! The bitch set my curtains on fire!"

The girlfriends rush to the bathroom where I hear water running and a lot of scuffling. After a moment Rae appears again, the charred curtain in her hand, her face flushed with anger.

"You're not the only one who's been through some shit."

The statement renders me oddly mute. At first, it sounds like some kind of emotional malapropism. As if she's incorrectly identified that what we're going through is the same, when really it's impossible for her to understand at all how I feel.

"For the record," she says, "the tattoo is in honor of my mother, who died a few years ago. Butterfly was her nickname."

She disappears into the kitchen. The men sit still, not moving, because they are cowards and because the world is backwards.

"I want to talk to my mother," I say suddenly.

Troy's face relaxes and then freezes, as if relieved and then caught. "A mother's love is wonderful," he says, and his gaseous phrase joins all the other gaseous phrases that permeate my head like sulfur.

"You are a human waste," I say to him.

Troy pales, looks sick. "What's wrong with you? You've gone totally dark on us."

"Margo goes Darko," Liam says, grinning stupidly. And the boys are looking at me anxiously. I guess I have that face on—that face that makes people anxious, like I'm going to lunge at Liam with the first object I can grab, stabbing and stabbing and stabbing until I've punctured something in the right place, and he can't breathe anymore, at which point I will sit back on my heels and watch him gasp for air violently until he dies. *That* face.

But instead I say, "Margo goes Darko." Then I say it again. "Margo goes Darko. Margo goes Darko." I say it over and over. The words pervade me with a wild, arcane sadness. I just keep repeating the line, not liking how it almost rhymes, but loving it, going crazy with that almost-rhyme, how it is so close but not, how it was never going to be, how it is a rhyme that was always degrading in its never was-ness, like me, like all those things from long ago, all the almost-truths in my life, like believing I could find an end to my loneliness, like believing my home was a place where there was love, and I think, *God, people, it was only ever burning, wasn't it, it was only ever falling toward the most down it could get, why did you never tell me this?*

Proxy Parenting Blues
Proxy Parenting Blues

I was helping my stepson Matthew with his homework when he asked me "Why carry numbers in multiplication?" The question seemed fair; couldn't we say twelve times five was fifty-something and call it a day? But I suspected this kind of reasoning wouldn't help him pass third-grade math.

"When you add larger numbers," I explained, "you have to carry the values. The sum of these two numbers is greater than nine so you bring the ten over to the left."

As a teacher, I should have had this tutoring thing in the bag. But he blinked at the worksheet, still confused. I tried to think of another way to explain it as Annie shuffled into the living room from play rehearsal, looking like she'd been slapped. This seemed promising, considering she usually looked like she'd been punched.

"Q and I broke up," she announced.

Annie and Q, whose real name was Quentin or Quinn or Quiver but who preferred to remain the singularly lettered man of mystery, had been in an endless makeup/breakup cycle since the spring play earlier that year. It was getting hard to drum up emotion around the whole thing.

"I'm sorry," I said. "What happened?"

"He says the general thrust of our lives are not the same. He says he just can't go where I'm going."

"Where's that—the girl's dressing room?"

"Maureen." She lowered her head at me like a bull about to charge.

"Ok, I'm sorry. I am. But you guys are constantly breaking up. You don't ever seem very happy with him. And maybe it might be nice to live the single life for a while?"

Her face contorted into a look that said the single life was about as nice as having your face eaten slowly by piranhas.

"I love him," she said.

"No."

Her mouth dropped open. "No?"

I didn't mean to say it. At least not so fast and with so much conviction. It was just a knee-jerk reaction to a surprisingly shitty new development—that my stepdaughter was in love with an insufferable thespian. This was the kind of guy who insisted on method acting for his role as Waiter #4 in last year's production of *Hello, Dolly!*

"Yes," she said. "I *love* him. He's my whole life."

I took a big sip of wine. This was worse than I thought.

"Annie, you're fourteen. Your whole life is ahead of you."

She sighed and removed her backpack.

"Unless you die early."

"Maureen!" she exclaimed, then turned away and sulked upstairs, making sure to drag her bag loudly over every step.

"You've got to work on your timing," Matthew said.

I had to work on a lot of things as of late, particularly this parenting deal. My husband, Hank, was in London for an annual software conference, and, at long distance rates topping eight dollars a minute, I was stepparenting in the isolation tank for the next ten days. This would have been fine, but since school started two months earlier, we were all losing our minds a little. Or at least, Annie was losing her mind, and I was catching some mutated strain of it, like the flu. Matthew seemed mostly content being nine and watching *Jurassic Park*, which had just come out on VHS, on a constant loop. Still, I felt a little outmanned by the boy who needed a teacher capable of teaching and a stepdaughter starring in a docudrama of her own life.

And then there was the first-name thing. Annie had always called me *Mom*, even before Hank and I got married three years ago. But calling me Maureen had grown some legs recently. It made me feel like some kidnapper. Even *Mother-by-Proxy* had a warmer ring than using my first name.

"Do you need more Dinosaur Juice?" Matthew asked, eyeing my near empty glass of wine. Since *Jurassic Park*, it was all things dinosaur around here.

"No," I said, pointing to his worksheet. "I need more multiplication."

Later, after Matthew went to bed, I checked in on Annie. She was flopped on the bed, phone to her ear, one of those clear plastic things with the neon-colored innards.

"Just saying goodnight," I said.

"OK."

"Did you finish your homework?"

"Yes." She had her hand over the receiver to block our conversation from the person on the other end. It was most likely Q.

"You know I was kidding about the dying early thing, right? That's very dark, and I probably shouldn't be saying those things. I was just trying to make you laugh."

"OK," she said, humorlessly.

I took a breath. "We need to talk about this whole love thing."

"I'm on the phone."

"The amazing thing about phones is they can be hung up."

I smiled. She did not. Why was I still attempting to use humor? My next idea was ripping the phone out of the wall, but I figured that would only pile on more drama, so I left and poured myself a little more Dinosaur Juice and sat in bed with the TV on mute. I could hear Annie in the next room over, but I couldn't make out what she was saying. In September, after much begging, we'd bought her a private line, and that seemed a mistake. The days of picking up the phone for some good old-fashioned eavesdropping were gone; now it was all muffled sounds thumping against the wall, my teen's emotions bouncing around so hard I feared they'd take the house down with them.

BY third period the next day, I was unusually tired. I taught tenth-grade English at Seneca, a public school one district over from the school Annie attended, lucky for her. We were reading *Macbeth*, which was generating a lot of interesting discussion in class. But today I was finding the Macbeth family dysfunction just a little exhausting on top of the home theatrics.

When the bell finally rang, I shouted out reading assignments as kids filed out, shouting their goodbyes to Mo-Flo. At first I feared the nickname was some variation of *motherfucker* fashioned from my name, Maureen Flowood; then one of my students explained it was because I was a mom who went with the flow. My sense of flattery was immediately supplanted by the fear that everyone would soon be on to me: I was actually in constant dread that my students weren't learning or listening and that they'd grow up to be underdeveloped citizens who eschewed things like literacy and civic duty and not leaving dogs in hot cars on account of me. But I didn't want them to know this, obviously, so I figured my only alternative was to hide out as Mo-Flo and hope no one sniffed me out.

The class had emptied, and I was erasing the board when I realized that Sally Krumbert was there, jutted up against my desk with her big stack of books. Sally had a way of just appearing, like an apparition but in black, platform shoes.

"Hi Mrs. Flowood."

"Hi Sally. What can I do for you?"

"I was wondering if you've seen the play *Cats*? My parents are taking me to see it. It's playing on Broadway."

"I have not seen that play. But I've heard it's a good one."

She nodded a few times. I waited for more, but there was only the awkward absence of follow-up. This was Sally. Smart, but odd. A bit of an X factor.

"Do you have a question about the reading, Sally?"

"'But screw your courage to the sticking-place, and we'll not fail!'" she shouted, pumping her fist straight in the air where it lingered long enough that I felt her point was overstated.

"Lady Macbeth," I said, dusting chalk off my skirt. "I guess that means you *don't* have a question about the reading?"

She shook her head and tapped a very methodical finger on her book.

"Everything else good?" I said. "Things OK at home?"

The question was a necessary—if not unnerving—precaution. When you inherited everyone else's kids for the better part of the year, remaining vigilant over actionable situations in the home was protocol. But more often than not, things weren't dire, so much as just crappy, and knowing what kind of shit parents were pulling on their kids only lent me more responsibility, with even less authority.

"Everything's fine," she said. "Do you know Brandi Copeland?"

I paused. I'd heard the name—a senior. I'd never had her in class.

"I do not," I said. "Not personally."

She nodded. Again, no clarification or follow-up content, just the tapping of the finger against textbook.

"Is there something I should know about her?"

"Oh. I'm thinking of saying *hi* to her. She's so cool. She's a senior. And it's not necessarily my right to say *hi* to her but I'm thinking of saying *hi* to her."

The second bell was going to ring, and I had to switch classrooms, but this kid was talking rights, for God's sake, when it came to simply talking to another human being.

"Hey," I said. "You can say *hi* to whomever you want. You're cool, and you have a fun style."

That last part made me cringe a little, but I thought it was something Mo-Flo would say. Sally's style, while certainly her own, was not exactly fun. She mostly layered herself in black, oversized items.

"Thanks, Mrs. Flowood. You're my favorite teacher. I just want to tell you that. My therapist says I need to find my voice, and right now my voice is telling me that you're a great teacher."

She turned and walked out. *At least there's a therapist involved*, I thought.

Dinner that evening was boiled chicken, boiled peas, and mashed potatoes out of the box. Another casualty of Hank's absence: decent meals. Hank is the cook; I manage only the basic Bs: boiled and boxed.

"How was school?" I asked the table.

"Good," Matthew said. "Mr. Hughes said the funniest thing today."

"What was it?"

He paused, chin up. "I don't remember. But it was so funny I couldn't stop laughing for twenty minutes."

"That *does* sound funny. Annie?"

"What?"

"How was school?"

"It was school." She dragged her fork across her chicken.

"Is the chicken terrible?"

She shook her head. The table was quiet. Silences at the dinner table deeply unsettled me. I always felt sharing our lives around a meal was the hallmark of a happy, functional family. Maybe if the Macbeths had opened up a little more over the spiced hen, that whole regicide thing could have been mitigated.

"So, how were things with Q today at school?" I asked.

Annie looked up at me, stricken. "Why would you ask that?"

"Because last night you were so upset."

"That was last night. It's all good now."

She went back to mutilating the chicken. What did *it's all good now* mean? Had she bribed him to come back? Had the thrusts of their lives miraculously realigned by homeroom this morning?

"We need to get my dinosaur costume for Halloween," Matthew said.

I turned toward him, realizing we were a week out with no costumes. This smelled like a very particular stepparent fail. I figured all those bio-moms had started hand-sewing costumes back in August.

"We can go shopping this weekend, K? What about you, Annie?"

"Halloween is for little kids," she said, pushing her chicken over to the other side of the plate.

"I see a lot of kids your age out and about. Who knows? I might even dress up."

"You could be a dinosaur!" Matthew said.

"She's not going to dress up as a dinosaur, Matthew," Annie said.

"I might," I said, winking at him. "Then we can match."

Matthew grinned. Meanwhile, Annie gave me a look like I had sucked her soul out of her body with a straw and spit it back in her face. The window for sharing time was closed, if it had ever really been open, and now I had a gnawing sensation that was chewing up any remaining appetite.

After dinner I folded a load of laundry that had been sitting in the dryer for three days and took it upstairs to distribute.

"Q and I are going to couples therapy," Annie told me, the moment I crossed her doorway.

"Oh?" I said. "And who is paying for this endeavor?"

"His sister is a psych major. She's going to do it for free, for the experience."

I sat down on the edge of her bed, where she was doing homework, and looked into her serious, brown eyes blinking out from under the thick, choppy bangs that she cut herself.

"Studying psychology doesn't mean you're ready to counsel a couple. Not to mention the fact that she's a family member, which is probably a conflict of interest."

"Whatever. Q says we won't survive without therapy. I have intimacy issues."

"What does that mean?"

"It means I have issues with intimacy. That's why we're gonna talk to his sister."

"This is a bad idea, Annie."

She stared at me before going back to her textbook.

"This is a *really* bad idea."

She shrugged, not looking up. "I have homework."

"Annie, I really . . ."

"I have homework."

She was giving me a busy signal. I could sit here, I thought, keep pushing, try to interrupt the signal, but I was afraid she'd just completely disconnect. Plus, truthfully, I was losing my nerve more and more these days, as if the kids, especially Annie, were getting older, wiser, and would soon figure out I was an imposter who had no earthly idea what she was talking about.

I woke up early the next day to the phone ringing. The caller ID flashed that it was Lucille, Hank's ex-wife. They'd split six years ago; Hank had won full custody. Lucille struggled with a mood disorder in the unspecified category, which meant she sort of ran the gamut as far as longitudinal emotional states go. In the last couple of years, she'd been on a mix of drugs that produced a more or less stable version of Lucille, though the meds seemed to do nothing to cut her general unpredictability and bouts of melancholy.

"I can't get a hold of Hank," she said, bypassing the hello. "I've been calling his office. He's not returning my calls."

"Hi Lucille," I said. "He's in London. He'll be back next Sunday."

"Oh," she said and went silent. I couldn't help but imagine the phone cradled between her head and shoulder, some soap opera on in the background while she filed the same nail over and over, having forgotten who she called and why.

"I want to take the children on a trip. Martha's Vineyard for spring break."

I was looking for something to wear in the closet but stopped, swallowing the urge to say something honest but regrettable. Which was that it was good that she was making an effort and yet there was nothing worse than her making an effort. This was a person who used to get lost going home from the grocery store, who locked herself in the bedroom when the kids were little. I tried to keep her recent strides as a saner person in mind, but the idea of the kids spending an entire week with her sent me into a low-grade hysteria that could easily have required my own prescription of mood stabilizers.

"I just think Martha's Vineyard would be fun," she said.

"I'm glad that you want to spend time with them, but are you sure a whole week is a good idea? Do you even know where Martha's Vineyard is?"

There was a pause. "Yes, Maureen, I know where it is. I'm not an idiot. And why wouldn't it be a good idea?"

I bit my lip. I was doing that thing I didn't want to do, which was to say something honest but regrettable.

"Why wouldn't it be a good idea?" she demanded.

"Listen, I'll have Hank call you."

There was a pause. "Well, can you tell Matthew I'll pick him up tomorrow at seven?"

"Your weekend with him was last weekend, remember? You canceled."

"But we rescheduled for this weekend. Matthew didn't tell you?"

She was getting that weepy tone that made me alternately want to calm her down with soft assurances and also punch her in the face. I mentally skimmed through the news dumps over the past few days for the update. Pajama Day coming up, a field trip in early November, yearbook pictures in two weeks. No mention of a reschedule.

"No, he didn't," I said, pulling from the closet a green blouse I was pretty sure I'd already worn this week. I decided that Mo-Flo's clothes liked to go with the flow of being worn twice.

"We did. We rescheduled."

"OK, I'll ask him. Maybe next time just keep your weekend, and this won't be an issue? Is it that hard to stick to the schedule of one weekend a month?"

I heard her take a breath and go silent. Retreat, Mo-Flo, I thought. I waited for the backlash of tears, but this didn't happen. Only a prolonged silence, which I decided was worse.

"Just talk to him and get back to me," she repeated and hung up.

MARK Pratt, the new guidance counselor, was in the department planning center when I got in at a little past seven. Everyone called him Pratt. He was a nice buffer against the existing guidance counselor, a perpetually sunny woman whose platitudes rendered her shark bait when it came to counseling teenagers who dined on counselors and platitudes.

"You're trespassing," I said.

"Coffeemaker's broken in the main office. Boy, do *you* look tired."

"Yeah," I said, as I poured a cup of coffee. "Tell me something. What do you tell your fourteen-year-old whose on-again/off-again boyfriend wants her to go into couples therapy with him?"

"Run? Like, really fast?"

"She *wants* to do it."

"Can you actually *tell* a teenager anything? I'm not sure their ears register the frequency of adult voices."

"I think it's a volume game. I just throw out as many words as I can before she walks away and hope something sticks. But I don't know. At least she told me about it. Right? She didn't have to. I have to believe on some level she wants to hear what I have to say. Not like it's going to change her mind."

"Would it really be that bad for her have a little therapy? Even if it's a session with a teenage dingbat?"

"His undergrad sister will be playing the part of the therapist."

"Oof." He tilted his head to one side to stretch his neck. "I don't know. I say this is part of life. We can't pad the world for our kids."

Exactly, I thought. And that's what's fucking killing me.

MATTHEW didn't want to spend the weekend with Lucille; he was too amped up for Halloween and wanted to go costume-shopping with me. I really didn't want to call her and break the news and thought maybe I just wouldn't, but my irritating good conscience had to weigh in. Lucky for me I got her machine, and she never called me back.

Finding Matthew's costume was the challenge I figured it would be—we drove all over town rifling through picked-over Halloween stores before finding a dingy T. rex costume in an outlet store an hour away. Annie was still diametrically opposed to Halloween, and I figured if she changed her mind, she was on her own.

"How is the show going?" I asked while driving her to an evening play rehearsal on Monday.

She was slumped against the window but made a small shrug.

"Well, I'm excited. I'm coming to every show and sitting in the front row."

"I'm just a chorus girl."

"You know what they say . . ."

"There are no small parts? That's completely not true. It's mostly only small parts."

"Still."

She sighed into the window. "I'm probably going to quit."

"What? Why?"

She kept her face turned toward the window. "Q's sister says I have abandonment issues. Because of when my mom went crazy. My bio-mom."

"You're quitting the play because you have abandonment issues?"

"No. That's just something else. Q's sister says that I need to learn to work through my issues, or it will effect every relationship for the rest of my life. She told me that I needed to confront my mother."

"What do you mean, *confront*?"

"She says that Mom lacks self-awareness and that I need to be a mirror for her so she can see herself. That's the only way for her to understand her behavior and then make amends. It's the only way to resolve the conflict between us."

I felt an apocalyptic panic spread over me, like she just told me she was going to walk out in front of a bus. The last time Annie took even a remotely confrontational stance it had ended very badly. During a visitation she'd asked Lucille why she was always late to pick her up, and Lucille burst into tears and didn't stop crying for two days. Annie came home afterward and locked herself in her room, finally emerging to say that she couldn't see her mother until she learned to be a better daughter.

"Annie, you know that you're always allowed to speak your mind, but you've got to think carefully about what it is that you want out of the conversation. Conflict resolution only works when both parties are willing. Talking to her with the expectation that she will respond a certain way could be very . . ."

"Are you saying my mom isn't willing to work it out with me?" Her face was off the glass now and aimed at me.

"It's not just about *willing*."

"You said *willing*."

"What I meant was *willing and able*."

"So you're saying she's not able?"

"I'm saying this won't go the way you think."

"What do you mean, *won't*? How do you know?"

I found myself tapping the brake as if it could somehow halt the momentum of this conversation and let us all back up a little. But what I'd said was out there, on the move, and Annie was breathing at me angrily, awaiting an explanation.

"What I mean is that it's complicated. Your mom has some complex struggles. I just think this is the kind of thing that should be discussed with a real professional. I will happily find you someone who is more experienced."

"Q's sister *is* experienced. She thinks I'm good for Q. That I can keep him on track."

Keep him on track? I stifled a scream as I turned into the school and threw the car in park.

"It is not a young woman's job to keep a man—let alone any other human being—*on track*. You are not his handler nor his coach nor his mommy. The little piss ant is responsible for himself. Do you hear me? Please tell me you understand what I'm saying."

She gave me a horrified look and then went for the door. I was going too far, but I couldn't stop advancing and reaching, as if I had to keep her from falling into an abyss with no safety line.

"Don't do anything before you talk to me, please? The play? Your mom? And think about a licensed therapist. Please? Can you promise me?"

She got out of the car. "I already have a therapist."

The door slammed shut. I watched her walk toward school, hunched over like some overburdened sloth. She wasn't the one lost in the abyss, I realized. I was, and she was walking away, deaf to my screaming.

CORINNE, one of my sixth-period students, was lingering the next day after class. Thin Corinne, was what the kids called her. For all her skinniness she seemed to have a lot of heavy thoughts weighing her down.

"So Landry and I broke up," she told me.

"Oh," I said, leaning against the desk. "I'm sorry to hear that."

"I didn't want to break up. He dumped me."

"Well, he's missing out."

"Do you think I'll find another boyfriend?"

She was still sitting at her desk, hands folded. She looked a little tense.

"I'm sure you will. But there's so much time for that."

She nodded a few times, her eyes drifting to the window. It could be Annie sitting here, I thought. Or even Sally Krumbert. I imagined locking all three of them in a room until they stopped obsessing about boys and seniors and focused on their own beings.

"I just can't wait until I'm married," she said.

"There's time for that too. There may be other things you want to do first, like college."

"Yeah," she shrugged. "If I even go to college."

I stifled a cringe. "Look, to be honest with you, getting married isn't the end-all-be-all."

"Are you married?"

"Yes, twice actually."

"So you liked it enough that you did it twice?"

She was deadpan. I tried to smile but ended up pursing my lips.

"My mom always says I'd be a great wife and mother."

This time I actually cringed.

"I'm sure she's right, but you're great at other things too. You're a great writer. And Mr. Donaldson says you're his best chemistry student. You've got this well-rounded thing going."

"Yeah, but so what? It's not like I'm going to do anything with it."

"Well, just keep your options, OK?"

What I really wanted to say was, *For fuck's sake, don't do what I did. Get married at twenty to a rageaholic.* I thought his intensity meant I was worth getting worked up over. I finally left him after the bookend he threw at my head came a little too close. Years later, after a little therapy and some hard growing up, I met Hank, the kind, gentle soul—with two kids. I was shocked to find that despite my deep void of maternal instincts, the package deal was alright.

But now I was worried that the kids got a raw deal, especially Annie, tossing about in the tumult with Q. I'd been afraid of not getting through to her, but maybe it was worse. I was getting through too much. Was it possible that I was only pushing her further down into the chasm of batshit craziness?

"I mean she was obsessed with infanticide," Corinne was saying.

Oh my God, what were we talking about? I blinked at Corinne.

"Lady Macbeth," she said, frowning at me. "She killed her own baby."

"Right. I think it's more likely that her child died in infancy."

"She hated being a woman. She rejected her own nature. She wanted to be unsexed. How can you reject your own nature?"

"It's complex, Corinne. I mean, you're tapping into a larger contextual conversation about motherhood in early modern England . . ."

"I *hate* Lady Macbeth. She's a terrible mother and a terrible woman and a terrible human being, and she should have killed herself earlier."

She's also fucking made up, I wanted to say. But Corinne was staring back at me as if to say *I know, Mo-Flo, that's exactly the problem. Actual parental bullshit is bad enough—why the hell saddle us with fictionalized family drama?*

MATTHEW came home that afternoon with a *D* on his math test. When he showed me he burst into tears and asked me if I was going to ground him for the rest of his life.

"Oh honey, of course not. I just think we need to get you a tutor."

"But I don't want a tutor. I want *you* to help me."

"I know sweetheart, but I'm clearly not helping you. You need someone who knows how to teach this better to you."

"Why don't *you* know how?"

I had no answer for this, which made him go flush with anger.

"Why don't you?" he demanded.

I let out a sigh as Annie stomped into the house to tell me she had quit the play.

"You already quit? We only just talked about this yesterday!"

She gave me a one-shouldered shrug, looking a little smug.

I rubbed a tired eye. "But you love the play."

"No I don't. It was just for my college résumé. I don't care about college anymore. Q and I are going to start our own business after school."

I stared at her, dumbfounded. "What business?"

"A restaurant. Asian fusion. Q's sister is going to be our business consultant."

There were no words. Annie stood there, eyebrows raised and arms crossed, waiting for me to validate this sudden display of entrepreneurialism.

"Annie," I said. "Running a business sounds a whole lot easier than it actually is."

"How do you know? You've never run one."

"Because it's not easy."

"So you *hate* my idea?"

"I don't hate your idea. But even if you were serious about this, you'd still need to go to college."

"I *am* serious about it," she said. "And that's why we have Q's sister. *She's* going to college."

"Bobby's dad owns a restaurant," Matthew said, suddenly cheered up by siding with Annie.

"See?" Annie said. "Bobby's dad did it."

She stared at me like she'd just landed the greatest argument of all time.

"OK," I said, throwing up my hands. "Open a restaurant. Go hog wild."

"Now *you're* not taking it seriously."

"I don't know what you want me to say, Annie."

"I want you to say you're on my side, Maureen."

"I *am* on your side."

"I want you to be on my side too!" Matthew said, thrusting his arms in my direction.

"I am *also* on your side. I'm on both of everyone's collective sides."

"Then I don't want a tutor," he said, throwing himself on the couch.

"OK then, we won't get you a tutor!"

"But then I'll fail!"

This revived the sob fest only with more flailing of limbs on the couch. Annie's body had gone limp like I'd shot a harpoon through her dreams. No one was going to move until I somehow said exactly the right thing that would make everyone happy. But Mo-Flo did not know the magical combination of words to make everyone happy. Mo-Flo was going to be the bad guy tonight no matter what she said.

After a fifteen-second stare-down with Annie to the soundtrack of Matthew's crying, I finally got up, stomped into the kitchen and pulled a tub of ice cream out of the freezer, grabbed a spoon, and started digging. The room went totally quiet for a long minute.

"What's that?" Matthew was up on his knees, peering over the couch.

"That," I said, pointing to the tub with the spoon, "is dinner. Come and get it."

They looked at each other unsurely and then hurried into the kitchen, eagerly grabbing spoons.

We stood around the counter, eating the ice cream out of the tub. This was such an easy and delicious dinner, I wondered why in the hell I had ever wasted time doing it any other way.

I was headed to the office the next morning to drop off paperwork when Sally materialized again, this time in stride with me, her huge pile of books clutched to her chest.

"I'm seeing *Cats* this weekend," she said. "I'm really excited. I would like to invite Brandi Copeland, but I don't know if she would go. Perhaps if she doesn't know me, she may not be inclined to take a trip into the city with me and my parents."

Reasonable, I thought. *Balanced. Way to go, Therapist.*

"Maybe you could take someone you know better?" I said.

"There isn't anyone." She sounded almost cheerful. "I'm going to say *hi* to Brandi at lunch though. Because I do have a right."

"Yes, you do."

We had stopped at the door to the office, where she lingered, staring into the glass door. Then she did an about-face and headed the other way.

"Have fun at *Cats*," I called after her.

Pratt was in his office with the door open; he motioned me in after I dropped off my paperwork with the admin.

"Did I just see you with Sally K?" he asked. He was stapling packets of paper. "Do you have her in class?"

"Yes. And out of class apparently."

"You know about that one, don't you?"

"She's a little different."

Pratt stopped mid-staple and made a face.

"What? Something else?"

"Apparently she was stalking some senior last year. Leslie Martin? Would follow her around in the halls but never approach her. Until one day she did. Rumor has it that she lopped off a chunk of Leslie's hair with a pair of scissors after luring her over to her house."

"*Luring?*"

"OK, so maybe that's a little strong, but either way, somehow Leslie ended up at Sally's house and then chop chop."

He made a scissor-cutting motion. I couldn't help but think of Brandi Copeland, the next unsuspecting victim in a nonconsensual haircut.

"Oh no," I said, dropping down in the chair across from his desk. "I think I'm an accomplice in her next crime."

Pratt lifted his eyebrows.

"She's fixated on some other senior. She's working up her nerve to say *hi* to her. I encouraged her to do it. She's going to induct the new Leslie."

I stared at him, horrified at the thought. Pratt frowned.

"Maureen, you're not responsible for Sally's actions. You know that, right?"

"Yes," I said, but I shook my head. "Where's my discernment when it comes to these things? I should have said something different. I should have told her to forget the senior and focus on loving herself."

"Then she'd cut her own hair off."

I looked at him skeptically.

"I'm kidding. Sort of. Look, this being a teenager—it's harrowing and weird, and I don't know how half of us survive. But we do. Some of us survive well, some of us not. Our job is only to vaguely steer them in the right direction. And I mean vaguely. This is just herding cats. Blind ones."

I liked that, *herding blind cats*. But I still felt like I desperately wanted to go tackle Sally Krumbert and cure her of this madness to turn teen girls into idols.

"You doing the Halloween thing?" he asked.

"Yep. Me and a dinosaur. You?"

"Ella's going to be a mermaid. Vivian spent the last two months sewing her costume."

"I knew it."

"Knew what?"

"Nothing. Your wife sounds awesome. I'll bet she can cook too."

"Are you comparing yourself to other moms? Is this what you're doing right now?"

"I just feel so, I don't know. *Spectacularly ineffective.*"

"I'm sure that's not true. But, in any event, don't worry about the Sally thing. You know how these things go. The ones you don't bet on end up surprising you. With all her ballsy initiative Sally will probably grow up to become a successful CEO or something."

"Or, with all this shady past," I said, "she'll go into politics."

HALLOWEEN was here. I wasn't going to be a dinosaur, which upset Matthew, but I dug out a pair of khaki shorts and a salmonish button-up polo and announced I was going as Laura Dern, which cracked him up. When we were all suited up to go bleed candy from the neighbors, Annie appeared in the hallway with a pillowcase.

"Are you coming with?" I said.

She nodded.

"What are you dressed up as?" Matthew asked.

"A virgin," she said, looking directly at me. My heart died briefly. "Just kidding. I'm going as a person who thinks Halloween is fun."

How meta, I thought. Well played.

We proceeded to trick-or-treat. It was a perfect October evening in Jersey, just cold enough to be crisp but not freezing. Matthew ran around like a dinosaur out of hell. Annie approached a few doors but mostly walked next to me quietly. The silent, subdued moment had me worried that we were missing an opportunity to connect, and now I had to decide which conversation took priority. Couples therapy bullshit? Asian-fusion restaurant ownership? The mother confrontation?

Before I could decide, Matthew ran back toward us, upset. His hood was coming apart at the seams around the neck, and he refused to go on until I fixed it, so I took him back to the house. I couldn't find my sewing kit nor any pins, but I did find a staple gun in the garage. When he heard the hard *phut* of the gun, he pointed at me, horrified, and accused me of animal cruelty.

"Matthew," I said. "It's not a real animal."

This only seemed to make him feel worse. "It is tonight! This costume sucks!"

"Can we just make do with this one? Next year I promise we'll buy you a better costume."

"Can't you make me one?"

"I don't know sewing like that."

"Do you know anything?"

I stapled a little harder, trying to talk myself out of being hurt and pissed while also simultaneously asking myself, because I couldn't help it, because I was actually constantly worried about the answer—*did* I know anything?

"Can you do me a favor?" I said, a little loudly. "Can you cut me a little slack?"

"What's that?"

"When you loosen up on the rope. You know?"

He looked at me blankly. I sighed and handed him the costume.

"It's just a thing you do when you love someone. You go easy on them."

He stared at the costume and then took it reluctantly and slipped it on. Annie had fallen asleep on the couch, but in my peripheral vision I could see her eyes were open. When I turned her way she closed her eyes again, as if she couldn't stand the thought of my look actually reaching her.

On Friday I returned graded Macbeth essays to the class. Corinne sat in the back, slumped in her seat. I had to call her name twice to come get her paper. She had written four pages on motherhood. The actual topic was Macbeth's visions and hallucinations. I'd given her an F. "See me after class?" I said after she came up to get it. She actually shrugged and pursed her lips as in, *Maybe, if I feel like it.* I watched her turn a cool back to me, incensed, trying to cover it up with my best Mo-Flo smile. But I could feel on my face it was too forced, too stretched, and I felt that this Joker affectation was probably blowing my cover, as I now officially looked as crazy on the outside as I felt on the inside.

Then, during lunch, Principal Fulton called me into his office. Pratt was in there too, and, from his face, it looked like he was trying to give me some telepathic message on what was about to go down, but there was not enough time for me to hear it.

What was going down was that earlier that morning Brandi Copeland told a teacher she felt threatened by another student—Sally Krumbert. Sally had been following her around for weeks until she finally approached her at lunch two days ago. Brandi asked Sally to leave her alone. The next day after school, on Halloween, Brandi found a dead hamster wrapped in a napkin on the hood of her car.

I listened, mortified, the blood drained from my face, and then recounted my conversations with Sally per Fulton's request. It didn't confirm much in terms of the dead animal, and the school was pulling security tapes from the parking lot to identify the culprit, but I felt sickeningly certain that Sally was our girl.

I white-knuckled it all the way home after the last bell, trying to tell myself it wasn't my fault. But it sure felt like my fault, at least partly. Mo-Flo with her casual advice to *go ahead and say hi.* Oh, and, if she rebuffs you, *gift her with a dead pet.* This whole thing only confirmed what I feared true, that even the in-control, disguised version of me was a hundred and eighty degrees out of alignment.

When I got home there was a message on the machine from Annie. Her mother was picking her up from school. She didn't say why, but I felt certain the confrontation was imminent. I paced the entire house from room to room while I waited, filling up three different glasses of Dinosaur Juice because I kept losing them. I'd succeeded in nothing except pushing Annie to do all the things I didn't want her to do. At some point Matthew turned on *Jurassic Park,* and I watched while I paced. I actually felt bad for the dinosaurs. They didn't mean to be a menace, they were just doing the only thing they knew, which was to chase kids around. Just like parenting. The problem was it's lose-lose. Either the kids escape your grasp or you catch them, only to eat them whole.

At 7:45 Annie walked in the front door. The moment she laid eyes on me she started crying. I sent Matthew upstairs, and then I hugged her for a minute and sat her down on the couch.

"What happened?" I said, rubbing her arm.

"I confronted her," she said, between sobs.

"Uh-huh," I said, gripping the top of her arm.

"It didn't go like I thought."

"Uh-huh." I gripped harder.

"Ow," she said, frowning at my hand.

"Sorry." I let go and took a deep breath. "What happened?"

She drew in a few labored breaths to slow down her crying.

"She was acting all strange when I got in the car. Like nervous that I wanted to see her out of the blue. She kept asking me what's wrong. She was worried and weird and kind of freaking out."

"OK."

"So it was already not going the way I planned it. Like, she already couldn't handle it or didn't want to sit down and hear what I had to say. She said that everyone's been coming down on her recently, and all she's doing is trying to be a mom."

I felt a sickening drop in my stomach, as if I'd just pushed both of us off a cliff. Lucille was talking about me. I'd actually greased the wheels for the confrontation to blow up in Annie's face.

"I just felt like I needed her to hear what Q's sister told me," Annie went on. "That I had issues because she had been absent or whatever."

She choked up again and started to cry quietly.

"Annie, I'm so sorry." I put my hand on her back. "I mean, I'm really, *really* sorry."

She looked at me, tears streaming. "I didn't end up doing it. I didn't end up telling her."

"You didn't?"

She shook her head and wiped her nose with the back of her hand. "I just told her that I loved her."

I blinked a few times. "You did?"

She nodded.

"You didn't confront her on all those other things?"

She shook her head. "No, I knew it wasn't right. Even before I went. She's not in that place, you know? She's not stable. So I didn't say it. Because it wasn't what she needed right now." She looked down at her lap. "She just needed me to loosen up on the rope, you know?"

I was stunned to hear my own words being echoed back to me. Stunned that the whole house didn't burst into flames because of it. We sat there for a few seconds before I went in for a hug, but she got up. The moment had passed, and now she had to go call Q. They were on the breakup circuit again.

I placed my own phone call to London. It would be late, but I wanted to hear Hank's voice, even if just for an expensive minute, even if just to let him know that things were bad all around but, really, they could have been worse. But the international line just kept ringing and ringing, not ever completing the connection.

Our Perpetual Lady of the Night

Monday night, Rae was just polishing off a bottle of wine at the home church meeting when the group got to prayer requests.

Mr. Loud Breather spoke up first, followed by the doe-eyed husband of Newly Married and Terrified, and finally Sexy Turtleneck, a busty woman always in tight turtlenecks, as if in a holy war with her sexuality. Since Rae could never remember anyone's name, she kept people apart through aptly appointed monikers.

Rae thought about tossing her own prayer in the ring. As an agnostic, such a thought was at least half sacrilegious in its own right, but after getting held up at gunpoint in the back of Hobbies and Stuff four months earlier, Rae's life had gotten weird enough to at least attempt to flag down a little help from above.

Rae's friend Lizzie, designated driver and unofficial caretaker, was giving Rae a worried, motherly look from the other side of the room. Rae hadn't asked to be chauffeured nor superintended, unofficially or otherwise, but Lizzie being Lizzie, she'd insisted. Their friendship had been an accidental union formed in sixth-grade biology when they protested frog vivisection. Now the two were an unlikely pair: the agnostic and the preacher's kid. *Confusing times all around*, Rae thought.

As prayer kicked off, Rae shifted her gaze to Rodney, the coworker who saved her life during the holdup. Rae had been following him to group for the past four weeks, hoping that, if there *was* a God, he would benevolently bless their union. She observed Rodney as he bowed his head, clad in a green and yellow sweater, a JCPenney-discounted gem that Rae found deliciously out of touch and disgustingly adorable. She wanted to lick his face. She wanted to take him straight home to her mother, with whom Rae had recently moved in.

Is there a dark horse in the running? was the way her mother phrased the question about men. There were a lot, actually, not so much in the running, just sort of all grazing about in her pasture, ever since her father had left two years ago for a woman he met in a laundromat. Rae avoided the topic of grazing horses since Mom was a strong Catholic with higher hopes for her daughter than meaningless sexual romps. Plus, Rae's grandmother was a loose woman who died of a questionable disease, so the whole promiscuity thing was a touchy subject.

But Rodney, the hero, was going to change all of that, Rae was sure. He knew what Rae had been through. If only Rae could get him to stop avoiding her. After prayer ended she waved to get his attention, but he had already started toward the door.

"Hey," she called after him, catching up with him in the hallway. Backed up against the staircase Rae couldn't help but notice how the green in his eyes sort of matched the green in his sweater.

"Hi Rae."

"Hey—how are you?"

"I'm doing well. And you?"

"I'm great. I've been trying to get a hold of you. I left messages on your machine. Did you get my messages?"

He nodded, a smile on his face. A smile that, like everything else in her life at the moment, was weird. Rae had a tendency to skew off-kilter these days, but she wasn't totally crazy, which was probably worse, because that seemed more predictable in a way. *Off-kilter* was like a viral weirdness you never knew when was going to flare up.

"I just thought that maybe we could hang out, sometime," Rae said, trying to sound casual.

"Yeah," he said. "I don't know. I think we should listen to Dr. Trimble. She said we need to be careful to avoid the trauma bond."

But that's exactly why we should be together, Rae wanted to say. We've been bonded by trauma.

"I know," Rae said. "I was there when she said it. Maybe coffee sometime? Just something low-key."

"Yeah," he said, "maybe."

Rae smiled, nodding, trying to *look* low-key so that her suggestion and her appearance all matched up, a feat that had become increasingly difficult to pull off these days.

And now her hand had somehow navigated to Rodney's forearm and was gripping it. Excitement and anxiety—identical twins as her therapist explained it—kept fooling her by trading places.

"We gotta go," Lizzie said, gently disconnecting Rae's hand from Rodney's limb.

Rae waved goodbye to him as Lizzie guided her toward the door and out into the car.

"This may sound mean," Lizzie said as she drove away like they were leaving a crime scene, "but you're coming off like an unhinged stalker-lunatic."

"Not mean at all. Lovely actually."

Lizzie bit her lip and went silent for a minute. Then said: "I don't know how to tell you this, but I've been asked not to bring you anymore."

"What? Why?"

"Well the drinking is a little bit of a thing."

"I thought that drinking was part of this new wave of the nineties twentieth-century church? We're allowed to get drunk."

"You're allowed to *drink*. In moderation."

Rae put both hands on the dashboard. "I can't believe you're uninviting me to church."

"It's not church, it's home group. And it's not me, it's Jim."

"Who's Jim?"

"The guy who leads the group."

Rae thought hard, trying to conjure up the face of the guy who led the group. "Man of a Thousand Tears or Personal Space Crowder?"

"Who or *who*?"

"The guy who cries *every* time or the guy who stands close enough to French kiss?"

"You've nicknamed these people?"

"Yeah, there's Vaguely Horrified Smiley Girl, Meatloaf Look-a-Like, Sexually Frustrated New Mom."

Lizzie pulled into Rae's mom's driveway and threw the car in park. "Do you have one for me?"

"No. You're my best friend. You're exempt from judgy nicknames."

"But for everyone else, it's game on?"

"Come on, those names are pretty balls on, right?"

Lizzie shrugged and nodded, suppressing a smile.

"I even have one for me. Our Perpetual Lady of the Night," Rae said, laughing. Then she hiccupped and leaned her head against the window.

Lizzie went quiet for a second. "That's not true of you."

"It is sort of," Rae said. "But I'm gonna turn things around. I think Rodney will be good for me. And maybe this whole church thing could be just what I've been needing."

"I think it's better if you stop coming," Lizzie said, softly. "It's not helping you. And I think you need to leave Rodney alone and work on your stuff. No more calling him."

Rae groaned into the window. There was this thing about Lizzie that drove her crazy. She said what Rae didn't want to hear in a way that made her actually listen. But right now Rae wished she was tone-deaf.

"Do you need me to carry you upstairs?" Lizzie asked.

"No."

"Seriously, are you OK? I could stay over."

"I have my mom," Rae said. "I'm fine."

"Well, you wanna go see a movie this week or grab dinner?"

Rae shook her head, feeling that thick melancholia eclipse her entire body. "I don't want to be a third wheel with you and Adam."

"You won't be," she said, quietly. "We're on a break."

Rae lifted her head from the window and looked at her. "What? Why?"

"We just are. Can I please help you upstairs?"

"No. I'm good. Swear."

"Rae . . ."

"I'm fine," Rae snapped, opening the door and climbing out, stumbling up the driveway, not looking back, even though she wanted to. She hadn't been so volatile before the incident. She just felt like she was coming apart. But she couldn't tell Lizzie that. Because once she started there might be no end to it. That's how bad it was.

Four months earlier, Rae was working late at Hobbies and Stuff, the craft-store purgatory of a job in a dumpy town called Atco. She'd just turned twenty, and as a birthday present to herself, quit community college for the second time. Christmas was coming and elderly ladies smelling of Jell-O mold were already getting rowdy over the tacky holiday decorations sprawling ten aisles of merchandise, which meant the employees were understaffed, buried in inventory, and pulling late shifts.

Rodney and Rae were in the workshop in the back, finishing up a custom-framing order. Someone was gifting five lucky recipients with an oversized, family Christmas photo, a plastic-looking group of five in red-and-green garb, plus a dog, donning his own Christmas sweater and a suicidal gaze. From opposite ends of a gigantic work table, Rae packed tiny spaces in the frame corners with putty while Rodney assembled frames. He was the only other employee in his twenties, but in Rae's two months of employment she had refused to acknowledge their common demographic if only because Rodney's banal sense of humor and dorky workman's tool accessory gave Rae a burning sensation she had entered the flames of social damnation.

"So what are your hobbies?" Rodney asked, without a trace of irony.

Rae's hangover had been zoning her out and producing visions of Bloody Marys. When she realized he'd just asked her a question, she blinked and shrugged. Conversation was clearly unavoidable.

"I don't know, guys and partying?"

"Cool," he said, though Rae suspected he did not think these hobbies were cool at all; she had already pegged him as a video-games-and-church kinda guy.

"I'm into gaming—computer gaming that is—and my church."

He paused there and drilled her with a look. Apparently, Rae was supposed to lob one back.

"Oh, which church?" Rae countered robotically, loathing that the laws of civility didn't allow a more individual expression like loudly yawning or completely ignoring him.

"Lakeway," he said. "It's a non-denom over on . . ."

"I know where it is," Rae said.

"Oh? Do you go to it?"

"I'm friends with Lizzie Harris."

He gave her a big smile, and Rae could feel his energy rushing her like an unwanted hug, the kind where your face gets smashed against some soft, sinkable bosom.

"I'm agnostic," she said, trying to break the energy.

But he only nodded. "You should come to our home group on Monday night. Anyone is invited. It's totally laid back. You're even allowed to bring beer or wine, if you want."

"How progressive," Rae said, returning to her putty-packing. After a minute she heard him slide off his stool and disappear in the back, probably to intercede for her soul. Cutting this whole thing short was now imperative, probably best accomplished by faking cramps. She would then have almost three full hours until last call at the bar in Clementon that never ID'd her. When she heard Rodney shuffle back into the room, she pressed her hand to her abdomen and bent forward, looking up. "You know, I'm feeling kind of . . ." But it wasn't Rodney who had come into the room. It was someone else. A man in a dark coat. He was not an employee. He was no one Rae recognized, in fact.

And he was holding an odd-shaped object. It was a gun. Pointed at Rae.

"Rodney," Rae called out, her voice oddly normal, as if someone was here to see him. Rodney was already in the doorway, frozen, one side of a frame dangling from his hand.

"Move into there," the man said, pointing with his other hand toward the office attached to the workshop.

"What do you want?" Rodney said, his voice desperate and terrible, not a voice Rae had heard before.

"Get in that room!" he said, thrusting the gun toward Rae.

Rodney turned and walked into the office like some kind of drone, and Rae followed, inching sideways so as to not turn her back on the intruder, as if taking her eyes off of him meant an instant shot in the back. He filed in behind them, and then the three of them were in the small, dank office, crammed up against a desk and some filing cabinets.

"Take off your clothes," the gunman said, looking at Rae.

Rae looked at Rodney as if for help, but he turned toward her, the light dimmed to nothing in his eyes. They were the eyes of helpless resignation.

"Take off your clothes," the gunman barked again, shifting the gun toward Rodney. "Or I'll shoot him."

The room went silent. Rae felt as if her heart had enlarged past her chest and expanded to the size of the room, as if everything that was happening in that room was now happening inside of her heart. Rae was dying, Rodney was dying, everything was dying inside of her heart.

Rae pulled the smock off slowly over her head and started to slowly unbutton her shirt.

"Take them off faster," he said, moving closer.

A little bit faster—though still slowly—Rae got to the last button, which was where she froze. She couldn't move. In a moment like this, all of the imagining what one might do in this kind of scenario dissolved into stark reality. The truth was that this moment, which was infinite, could only be held inside the space of Rae's utter lack of control, which was even more infinite.

"Take off your clothes, slut," he said. Then, as some kind of necessary afterthought: "You're just another slut."

Rae felt a warm, sharp kick inside. She wouldn't know this until later, but what was actually happening was that she was in labor. An inward delivery of shame. That word, *slut,* how it pierced her immediately, how it drilled straight to the core of who she was and gave it a definitive name.

"Hurry up!"

"Please," Rodney said, and now his voice was floating around within the space of her heart too. "Don't do this."

"Shut up," the gunman said, moving closer, almost touching Rodney's chest with the gun. And at that moment there was some noise outside—a dog barked, a car passed, a fly hiccupped—who knew. Whatever it was tripped up the rhythm of the moment and tore open a tiny hole of opportunity in which the gunman turned slightly, and Rodney batted the gun away and lunged for the man.

After a struggle that ended with the guy hightailing it out without his gun, Rodney stood, transformed before Rae's eyes into a celestial hero-being, and Rae, her last button intact, thought *Dear God if you're there, I have been lost but now I am found.*

VALENTINE's Day was coming, and Hobbies and Stuff had exploded into a nauseating sea of pink and red. Rae had the luxury of stocking candy hearts at the registers and unpacking scads of Valentine's merchandise. Since Lizzie seemed to be on perpetual weekend retreats recently, Rae had picked up extra shifts and even covered for the old-lady employees when they needed to go to a funeral or some grandkid's birthday party. It's not that she liked it there. In fact, she carried a newfound repulsion for the place. But she couldn't leave it for some reason. What would leaving do for her anyway, since she couldn't escape what happened to her that evening no matter where she went? More importantly, it kept her close, in a way, to Rodney, even though he'd quit at the end of December.

For a few weeks after the incident, Rodney and Rae had stuck together. They talked on the phone or at her apartment, recounting the incident, or *processing*, as the therapist called it. Hobbies and Stuff had donated the therapist for free, most likely to ward off a lawsuit. Rae went to a few sessions by herself that seemed like she was being forced to live it all over again, only this time alone. So she asked Rodney to go with her, and the pain became just a little more diffused, a little more manageable. After he attended a few sessions with her, the therapist mentioned trauma bond, which promptly ended their sessions together. Then Rodney slowly stopped coming around at all, and Rae's apartment loomed with a scary kind of emptiness, so she hauled a bag of clothes over to her mom's and made up a lie about a fire at her apartment.

Rae couldn't tell her mom about the ordeal. Surely, between the unexplained absence of a social life, the uniform of oversized sweatshirts, and the dull torpor in her voice, Mom must have detected something was amiss. But since Rae's dad's laundromat mistress had died in a freak accident six months earlier—she'd literally been flattened by a bus—telling Mom seemed precarious. Rae feared a belief in her mother that negative occurrences in a person's life were a direct and karmic result of that person's bad deeds. The last thing she needed was Mom confirming that Rae was transitioning into adulthood rather irresponsibly and that perhaps the gunman had been sent by the cosmic forces to deliver this very message.

"No plans?" her mother asked from the living-room doorway on yet another Saturday night for Rae of cable and vodka tonics.

"Don't feel like going out," Rae said, trying to sound as if she was actually in control of her destiny anymore.

She watched three movies in a row, the last of which was a predictable romantic comedy about a girl and guy who just couldn't seem to get it together, until the end, where they ended up in a diner, laughing about their entire movie of problems, as if all anyone needed was a little coffee and pie. Mom, who joined her halfway through, cried, which made Rae feel depressed. Then Mom went to bed, which depressed her even more.

Rae poured herself another vodka tonic but held the tonic. She felt boxed into an unlivable space. And now that she had gotten kicked out of church group, she felt boxed *out* as well, which made her feel slammed between two totally different but equally bad places. She wanted to call Rodney, but the lingering fear that she might actually be a stalker stopped her. All she wanted was some reality where the two of them made sense; otherwise it felt like her world was hopelessly turned upside down.

She pulled out her old day planner that she'd bought for school but ended up mostly using to write down phone numbers. After Rae had gone into hiding, her social network had mostly dissolved. The last person she'd seen was Neil, a bartender she was sort of seeing before the incident. She had also at one point been seeing Neil's roommate and, before that, Neil's roommate's best friend, Kurt.

Rae lifted the phone receiver from the end table next to the couch, her fingers hovering over the numbers. A vague anxiety was lurking somewhere far-off. She punched in seven digits before she could think twice. The machine picked up. She left a message with her mom's number. Then she circled the living room, waiting for a response, slamming two drinks in the interim.

After twenty minutes Neil called back: "It's you! Come over and see my supercool new place."

Rae dug a less oversized shirt from the bag of clothes she was living out of in the guest room, along with some black pants, slapped her cheeks a couple times to look alive, and navigated her way to the address Neil gave her.

She pulled into his parking lot and walked up the stairs to his condo, feeling her stomach twist into an unfriendly shape. This is normal, Rae told herself. Going out is normal. There's nothing wrong with this. But when Neil answered the door shirtless, the sudden urge to vomit all over his six-pack abs seemed decidedly not normal.

"Rae! In the flesh!" he announced, grinning. He over-hugged her and then let her into his place, which, sure enough, was supercool. Rae followed him around while he pointed out his cool stainless steel appliances, his cool abstract art on the wall, his cool modern furniture. He was still rooming with John, who was there with Kurt, incidentally, the two playing video games in the living room.

They circled back to the kitchen where Neil poured whiskey into two glasses with ice.

"Such good timing. I was just staying in and chilling tonight."

This was code for getting shit-faced at home, instead of at the bar.

"Seriously," he said handing her the glass. "Where have you been? We all thought you got abducted. Or joined the Salvation Army or some shit."

Close, Rae thought. *Very, close.* "I've been around."

He shook his head, grinning. "Woman of mystery."

"Keep 'em guessing, is what I always say."

Rae took a big drink to make herself stop talking. Is this what she sounded like? She kept the glass at her lips to stall. She had absolutely nothing to say. Had she ever? What in the hell had she ever had to say?

Neil reached across the island and pawed playfully at her belly. Rae tried not to retreat. After all, she knew what she had been getting into when she came over. Drink, flirt, screw, repeat. This was what dating was, right? Looking for the right guy, the right relationship? But how would you identify the right one when they all essentially looked the same, were all directly interchangeable?

Because really there had been many Neils that Rae had run through the cycle in the past two years. And the thing that made her want to curl up on the floor and never get up was that the guy with the gun had her number. She had fashioned herself into just another slut.

Her drink was empty. Neil was pouring another, chatting about something. Rae felt hostile introductions being made in her stomach. Vodka, meet whiskey. Whiskey, meet vodka. She tried not to dwell on the fact that she had slept with literally everyone in this apartment. She didn't want to do this all over again but here she was, doing it. She didn't want to be a kid, running from something, running away from what her dad did, being reckless and disloyal, only to find that she was actually running in the same direction, being reckless in a way that was exactly like her father.

Neil held the refilled glass out to her. "Should we get you out of those clothes?"

He grinned. Rae answered him by vomiting all over herself.

AFTER sleeping off the alcohol on Neil's couch and driving home before sunrise so Mom wouldn't see her come in, Rae showered and dragged herself into work at seven A.M.

She was on sale-item duty, which meant taping up fifty-percent signs on the ends of all the aisles that had sale items. Thirty seconds after they'd opened, an old woman with a cart already full of Valentine's crap was accosting Rae in the wicker aisle.

"Is the wicker on sale?"

"Yep." Rae tapped the paper. "That's what the sign says."

She picked up a set of nested wicker baskets.

"Can I just buy one?"

"They're nested. They go together. We have single baskets over there." Rae pointed to another shelf with single baskets.

"But I just want one."

"They're nested," Rae said again.

"I just want this one." She jiggled the wicker basket that was secured to two bigger baskets with a plastic tie.

Rae stared at her wrinkly face. "Fine." She pulled her box cutter out of her back pocket and cut the plastic ties on both sides, then handed her the basket. "There's your one."

"How much is it?"

"I don't know," Rae said, throwing her hands up. "I don't know how much it is. It's not an actual item. It goes with these." Rae shook the other two at her. "Go ask someone up front."

The woman shuffled away. Rae hated this place and all of its dumb customers. But cutting that plastic felt strangely satisfying. Taking it apart was a strange relief. She wandered back to the framing section, the only part of the store she purposely avoided. Oversized framed photos were stacked against the wall, waiting for customer pickup. Rae ran her hand on a framed picture of a family in matching shirts. They looked happy, in a checked-out way. Maybe that was the only way to be happy.

Rae put her hand on the corner of the frame that had been puttied, remembering that coming-apart terror she felt when she first saw the gun pointed at her. She pulled at the corner, separating the wood a bit. Pulled it more until the wood split and tore away from the photo. *Tear it up*, Rae thought. *It's going in that direction anyway.*

So Rae dragged her box-cutter down the entire photo. Several times.

By the time a coworker got back there the entire frame shop looked like some crime scene after a custom-framed-photo serial killer had passed through.

Rae holed up in the house and didn't answer the phone. She didn't need to hear that she was fired. She was fine with just not going back to work. She didn't want to hear anything, especially Rodney's calls not coming through.

After a few days Lizzie showed up in her room.

"Have you not gotten my messages?"

"You've emerged from the bowels of the church retreats, I see."

Lizzie looked around the room at encrusted bowls of mac & cheese and empty vodka glasses. "When was the last time you left the house?"

Rae shrugged again.

"Get dressed. You're coming to the women's event with me."

"The women's what?"

"The women's event at the church."

"No, I'm not."

"Yes, you are. You're not staying here."

"I'd rather go to my own execution," Rae said.

"This will be very similar," she said, grabbing Rae's sweater from off the chair and tossing it at her.

In all of the years Rae had known Lizzie, Rae had only grazed the outside of Lizzie's father's church. She had never actually gone inside the building. Tonight they ended up in a big banquet hall where round tables had been set up in a gigantic cluster around a stage. A long foldout table stretched along the back wall; on it were tiered dishes with various finger foods. A fountain of bubbly stuff capped off the display at the far end. Rae guessed sparkling cider. Her skin was starting to crawl a little. She had a sudden ravenous hankering for a bloody steak and a cold six-pack.

A crowd of women was migrating toward Lizzie. Rae trailed her as they worked their way toward the stage, feeling quite certain that the eyes and pressed smiles turned toward Rae regarded her as nothing more than some sad stray animal that had followed Lizzie here.

They landed at a table right up front next to the stage, where Lizzie's mother was getting prepped with a mic. She regarded Rae with a disoriented look of shock, probably because Rae was actually present in church, but then the look settled, and Mrs. Harris waved warmly. Rae had always like Lizzie's mom; as pastor-wives went she was enthusiastic but not pushy, at least not with Rae. Lizzie was a different story; Lizzie's mother often fought with her about her involvement in church and the perpetually stalled engagement to her boyfriend, Adam. It's not that Lizzie and her mother were exactly at polar opposites on these issues—Lizzie wanted to be involved in church, just not so much church. And maybe, as Rae thought about Lizzie's current break with Adam, she wanted to be with Adam, just not so much Adam.

Mrs. Harris got up on stage, made a few announcements and introduced the special guest, who then took the stage. She was the wife of some pro golfer who had a to-hell-and-back story involving drugs, teenage pregnancy, infidelity. In some ways it reminded Rae of her own testimony: left by dad, college dropout, boy-crazed bar-hopper. Held-at-gunpoint survivor.

Rodney-saved.

There it was again, what seemed like the pivotal moment of change in her life. And yet, somehow she was still waiting to pivot. She glanced around at the women in the sanctuary sitting with a kind of quiet eagerness. How many of them had done bad things? Were any of them like Rae, wandering and carousing and trying to grow up but finding that it was nothing but wasted weeks piling up? Had anyone had a complete stranger with a gun look straight into them and tell them exactly who they were? She felt that familiar unstable feeling, that violent coming apart. She turned toward Lizzie for some kind of help, for something. Lizzie was staring off into the crowd, looking rather flat, not quite right. Rae grabbed her hand. Just as she did, Lizzie shot out of her seat and walked straight for the door.

Rae hesitated, wondering if maybe Lizzie was just headed to the bathroom. But she was walking too fast. Rae stood up and followed.

By the time Rae got outside, Lizzie had walked past her car and was heading for the road. When Rae called her name, Lizzie slowed, then stopped and turned. Rae did a little jog until they were within arm's reach of each other.

"What's going on?" Rae asked, searching her face, which was both white and dark, in and out—an entire system of contradictions which Rae couldn't see her way through.

"Oh fuck," Lizzie said, finally, throwing up her hands. Rae held her breath—if Lizzie was cursing, it was bad. Really bad. "I cheated on Adam."

"Oh my God," Rae said, grabbing Lizzie's arms, as if to keep her from floating away. "Wait, what do you mean, *cheat?*"

"I mean I slept with someone who isn't Adam."

"Oh my God," Rae said, louder, releasing Lizzie and grabbing her own arms, as if Rae was the one who was going to float away. "But you haven't even slept with Adam."

"Tell me about it."

"Well, who was it?"

"Some guy I met on a retreat." She dug one palm into the space above her eye and rubbed. "I'm so stupid."

Rae couldn't imagine her sneaking around with Retreat Guy, trading in her V-card in the bunk bed of some mothballed cabin.

"I don't understand," Rae said.

"I don't either." She stared off into the middle distance. "I'm supposed to be all these things that I'm not."

The moment she said that, Rae realized she very much did understand. She understood that Lizzie could be stupid and impulsive with a guy to whom she was attracted and who was attracted to her, a guy who made her feel something she desperately wanted to feel, or else offered relief from something she wanted to stop feeling.

"So what happens now with Adam?" Rae asked.

"Well *that*'s probably over. Once I tell him, anyway."

"He doesn't know?"

"No way."

They stared at each other. They were locked in a complex puzzle of reversals, a labyrinth in which they had both been working from opposite ends, only to bump into each other and find they were both trapped.

"Why didn't I know any of this?" Rae asked.

Lizzie bowed her head and stood, drawn into herself, perfectly still. Whether it was the silence of prayer or the silence of grief, Rae didn't know.

Then Lizzie looked up at Rae. "You've had some stuff going on."

"I'm sorry," Rae said, feeling for the first time in a while a pain attached to the hurt she'd inflicted on someone else, as opposed to herself. "I've been a bad friend. I've been self-involved and crazy, and I'm sorry."

"It's not like you haven't had a reason," Lizzie said sadly. The sadness, Rae knew, was for both of them to share.

Lizzie bowed her head and drew in again. Rae's hands came to rest on Lizzie's arms, gently. It occurred to her then that the silence of prayer and the silence of grief were exactly the same thing.

LIZZIE dropped Rae off at home. She was going to tell Adam the next day and asked that Rae send up a prayer or a wish or however Rae communicated with the universe. "I usually send a fax," Rae told her, which got them both laughing.

Inside, Rae found her mother on her hands and knees in the hall closet, tossing stuff into a box.

"What are you doing?"

"Cleaning," she said, emerging with a pair of brown slippers. "Your grandmother wore these everywhere! Even the grocery store. They used to be white. Do you want these? Not to wear, necessarily, just to have."

"Nasty. No. Why did you keep them?"

She shrugged and threw them in a box as Rae wandered into her mother's room. There was a pile of stuff on the bed as well—some old clothes, costume jewelry that belonged to her grandmother. Rae picked up a pair of clip-on earrings and put them on, examining herself in the mirror. According to pictures, Rae looked a lot like her grandmother—was named after her, in fact. She had gotten pregnant when she was fifteen by an older man who left her in the delivery room. Alone with the new baby, she scratched out an impoverished existence. She'd shack them up with men who would buy them food and pay the rent, and by thirty-four, she was sick. She nicknamed Rae's mother *Butterfly* to represent the power to transform ugly things into beautiful things.

Rae laid down on the bed and listened to her mom digging around in the hall closet. On the dresser was some stuff of her dad's—an old watchcase, a cigar cutter, some handkerchiefs. Rae hadn't spoken to him in several months. This was the only stuff left behind.

"Do you think that Dad got what was coming to him?" Rae called out to her mom.

"What do you mean?" she called back.

"That laundromat mistress's death. Do you think God was punishing him?"

There was a silence. Then Mom appeared in the doorway.

"Since when do you believe in God?"

Rae propped herself up on her elbows. "I didn't say I didn't. I just didn't say I did. That's kind of what an agnostic is."

"I see," she said, crossing her arms and sitting on the bed. "I don't know that punishment works that way with God."

"Really? You don't think that getting flattened by a bus is some kind of cosmic payback for stealing someone's husband?"

"I think getting flattened by a bus is bad luck."

"What about Grandma? Do you think she got what was coming to her for, you know, being a lady of the night?"

"I don't know that I can speak to what was coming to her, Rae. She was just a person who did the best she could and made mistakes, like all of us, I guess." She frowned at Rae. "Where did you go tonight?"

"I went to church."

"Is that a euphemism for something?"

"No. I went to church with Lizzie. It wasn't as churchy as I thought it would be. There was a lady who talked about all the bad shit that happened in her life. I kind of liked her."

"Interesting," she said. "How is Lizzie?"

"Good," Rae lied, though she really wanted to say the truth—any truth really—as if some spirit of confession had touched her. She wanted to confess her own dark secret, that what the intruder had said about her was accurate. That he had aptly named her.

"There's a guy I like," Rae said instead.

"Oh?"

"Or, think I like. He's a church guy. He's nice. He's the only boy who has managed to keep my clothes on."

Rae laughed. Her mother's face fell a little bit.

"It's a joke, Mom," Rae said, but she was lying. It wasn't a joke at all.

"I really hope that you're being careful," she said quietly.

"Why, because bad things happen to bad people?"

She paused, her face a little stricken. "No. Because I love you, and I think you are not so kind with yourself. Do *you* think you're a bad person who deserves to be punished?"

Rae said nothing. But the answer was *yes*. Because she'd not been kind to herself. She'd been reckless. And it was the gunman who had come to punish her but Rodney who had saved her from having to pay the full penalty. Is that why it felt like Rodney was her only hope?

THE next day Rae drove over to Games and More, the video game place where Rodney was working now. He was chatting with some kid by the register and didn't see Rae when she came in, so she crawled along the far wall, perusing the rows of video games. A succession of games with covers of battle-worn soldiers, anime rat packs, and cartoon characters in racing vehicles climbed toward the ceiling like a stampede—as if they were going to crush the life out of her.

"Rae?"

Rae turned. Rodney stood a few feet off, stationed by an endcap. His workman's tool was still clipped into his belt.

"Hi."

"What are you doing here?" he said, blinking nervously.

"I need to talk to you."

He glanced around the store, either taking inventory of customers or looking for an out, then looked back at her, clutching at the workman's tool on his belt.

"Alright."

"Alright," Rae said, trying to locate what, exactly, she wanted to say. "I know I've been acting a little crazy, but I just feel like you're the only one who can possibly understand. You were there."

"I know," he said. "But I don't know what you want from me."

"You saved me. Do you understand? And it just feels," she paused, waiting for a small truth to untether itself, a truth that once uttered, would somehow get her where she was trying to go—a world where it was safe, where her heart was not so enlarged and unmanageable and too filled with terror. "It just feels like love."

The words surprised her. They were a truth, just not the one she was expecting. They were a truth that had nothing to do with Rodney and everything to do with her. The world was not safe, it was dangerous, not just because of its random, senseless violence, but also because she'd been searching for something *like* love, not actual love. Dangerous because she'd come to believe that she deserved only a counterfeit and not the real thing, and this was the real terror.

Rodney was absolutely silent. A silence so massive, so infinite, one that would never be filled, that would just keep expanding infinitely, a God-silence. There was nothing more to say. Rodney had saved her life, and there would never be enough gratitude. But to keep saving Rae was not possible, not his job, and not the point anyway.

He looked down, his hand still clutching at his tool. She turned and walked out the door, into the cold, February air where she stood for a moment, her hands pulled into the arms of her sweater, one of so many that she had bought, not because she was close to converting but because she wanted to cover herself up, hide the shame. Then Rae thought of Lizzie, breaking the news to Adam, possibly at this very moment, and found herself lifting something up to the air. A kind of wish that despite Lizzie's terrible confession, Adam would still be kind to her, would not utter something that would in any way speak condemnation of her for just being a person, just being a woman, who was doing her best to survive and feel loved in this world.

And this thing she was lifting up on behalf of Lizzie reminded Rae of what her mother told her when she was younger, that a lady always guards her heart and how really what she was saying—entreating—was *please, please, please don't let anything rob you of your beauty, don't let anything devour your lovely interior, especially your own difficult reproof, let that loveliness remain, let yourself let it remain, in perpetuity, let it remain.*

GRIEVING A LIFE OF WATER

It's Halloween. Vivian is upstairs in a bathtub with no water, where she has been since it turned dark. Her Pharmie Army, as she calls her antidepressants, is holding the front line, behind which she can remain dulled and bunkered from the witches and monsters and princesses begging for candy. I am downstairs with our children, Jack, six, and Marion, seven, who are masquerading as Spiderman and Cinderella, respectively. They watch *The Little Mermaid* on the couch, both eyes going wide as Ursula, the seductively scary sea witch, appears on the screen. They are both transfixed by the cartooned version of the larger-than-life octopus romping about in the deep sea with her vampy blue eye shadow. My mental index of sea-life trivia contains a random fact about the octopus: it's nicknamed *devilfish* for its sinister appearance.

There is the surface, and there is everything underneath. On the surface is the daily inertia of our lives, going to work, feeding the children, managing through holidays such as this one. But we don't really live here on the surface; we live underneath in the deep trenches, where our oldest daughter's kidnapping, five years earlier, remains unsolved. Down here all of the questions disappear into the deep drop-offs where answers are too dark and too deep to be found.

The doorbell rings. Jack and Marion scramble off the couch, eager to see costumed crusaders. I place my scotch on the table and force myself up, grabbing the candy bowl from the table just before opening the door. Jack and Marion assume a position by each leg. To my children, Halloween is an intriguing event of sugary otherness, one night when the world is a parade of characters they get to watch while consuming concessions. At the door is a group of high schoolers, who, as usual, have turned out a weak costume show, putting in half-assed efforts to meet the minimum requirement of a Halloween trick-or-treater. Pillowcases are thrust toward me; these have replaced plastic pumpkin buckets in order to ensure maximum candy collection. I drop miniature chocolate bars into half-filled sacks belonging to a girl with a pacifier around her neck, another one with a bachelorette sash, and a boy wearing a black mask around his eyes.

"What are you?" I ask him, dropping a Snickers into his bag.

"A bandit," he says flatly, as if I've already overstayed my welcome in my own doorway.

"Oh yeah?" I raise an eyebrow and move into the doorway a little more, filling up the space. "What do you steal?"

He stares back at me through his mask, a cheap plastic thing he probably picked up at the Dollar Store. "I dunno. It's just Halloween, man."

In my previous life, before Ella went missing, I was a high school guidance counselor and a good one at that. I could go twelve rounds with an ornery teenager before I even thought about breaking a sweat. But in this moment I envision myself ripping the mask off his face and pulling him toward me by the collar until we're face-to-face in a kind of involuntary near-kiss, a scotch-and-rage-induced encounter that would let him know that I *know*, more than his hormonally unhinged, underdeveloped brain could ever understand, that it's *just Halloween, man*. As if this night, the last night we had with Ella, isn't stitched crudely across every square inch of my skin, cobbling me together like some horror-show marionette. A night we allowed Ella, in a homemade mermaid costume that Vivian spent a month sewing for her, to trick-or-treat for the first time with a group of her friends, no chaperones.

The kid's beady eyes are staring at me. I can feel an anger within me mature so quickly it's already ancient, as if here long before I was. I'm aware that Jack and Marion are watching and waiting for something they feel but can't describe, for their father to come apart, finally. But because I have salvaged a tattered remnant of sense that I must protect my children, I wave my hand at the group, shooing them away, harshly, but for their own good. For everyone's own good, really. Then I move back from the doorstep, shutting the door, putting a solid piece of wood between those kids and me.

But I keep my palm against the door, while Jack and Marion flit back to the couch, and I think of Vivian upstairs in the tub, like some kind of mermaid-turned-human, grieving a life of water, a life once connected to the core of her being, now taken from her.

I FIRST saw Vivian on a beach in Mexico after returning from a dive trip. She was laying out by the water with some friends. I stood on the dock, just off the boat, staring like an idiot until one of her friends noticed me and gestured in my direction. Vivian turned and tilted her head, squinting, as if she was trying to place me. I waved. Her friends laughed, but she just stared, curious, for several seconds, before looking away again.

I washed and hung my diving equipment, ate lunch at the pool bar, and went for a swim, remaining vigilant of her whereabouts all afternoon. Eventually she was alone, packing up her things. I approached her.

"Ever been diving?" I asked. She shook her towel out and then folded it but didn't look at me. "Can't tell if that's a *yes* or *no*." I dipped my head to try and catch her eye.

She stuck the towel in her bag and picked up her sandals, shaking the sand from them, then started walking away from me, toward the hotel.

"It's incredible," I said, right on her heels. "You're breathing. Underwater."

She continued up the path. I followed her for a few more steps and then pulled up right next to her so we were walking side by side.

"The first time I went down there, I looked up under the surface and thought, I'm underwater without the pain in my lungs of holding my breath. It was a total trip."

She picked up her pace a little. I did too.

"I kept thinking," I went on, "I shouldn't be this far underwater, breathing. Which made me want to stop breathing. But then I realized, I was fine. I found my breath where it shouldn't have been."

We had arrived at the hotel entrance. She stopped and looked at me, her whole face drawn into a frown.

"I'm Mark Pratt," I continued. "But everyone calls me Pratt. What if I took you on a shore dive, right off the reef? You don't have to be certified. Then afterward, dinner."

She tilted her head and examined my face. "Are you this terrible at taking hints or what?"

"Oh my God," I said, as my head and shoulders went limp. "It's that obvious?"

She looked down at the shoes in her hand and shook her head. Then she raised her eyes, and we exchanged a look that only people who know each other do. At that moment, from the outside, we must have looked like a couple having a fight. She took in a deep breath and let out the longest sigh. A long surrender. I would hear that sigh many times, especially when it came to Ella, our firstborn, whose tenacity and magnanimity was so big and bright that it amazed and exhausted and confounded us, and we simply could not remember how we'd ever lived before she came into the world.

AFTER the movie trails off into end credits, I put the kids to bed. They want to sleep in their costumes, and who am I to stop them on such a night; this is the last night they saw their sister. It's their loss too, though they will have a drastically different memory of such loss. I can't say what they will remember when they are grown—maybe Ella will only feel like a vaguely intimate stranger they met for a while, a person they will always remember but never really know. I kiss them both goodnight, mouth dry and ready for another scotch so as to blot out this thought of my younger children as adults. It's the kind of thought that's cropped up recently, a foreshadowing of a dark reality, one without Ella. I could have Vivian kiss them goodnight—she would do it if I asked—but by now she has probably amassed a chemical combination to which I'd rather not expose the kids. Not on this night. I turn off the light in the old craft room, which is where they now sleep together. It's closer to the master bedroom. After the taking, I installed double vent window locks and a security system on the windows. There's a double key deadbolt on all doors now and a camera in every room and the main hallway. The therapists told us that paranoia was normal, that an intense, animal-like protectionism over the other children would arise, giving us a false sense of control, but that it was important to come through it so as not to entrap ourselves in a prison of fear or, worse, to put this fear into the hearts of the kids.

But what of our hearts, and what has been put in them? That vessel has become an endless, terrifying sea in which our daughter has been lost. I return back downstairs. I don't bother with the glass; I just grab the bottle from the bar and park myself in the chair. *The Little Mermaid* is playing again on TV. The story of a little girl willing to give up the sea to walk on the land as a human. Ella wanted the opposite, to transform from a human into a mermaid and swim through the neighborhood, knocking on underwater doors for treats. It was only supposed to be for one night. She was not supposed to be carried off into the sea, dragged away by some devilfish to a place among the beautiful phosphorescent life that is so deeply out of our reach.

She vanished on the way home from the bus stop the day after Halloween. In an instant, people and things attached to us multiplied. Added to our lives were detectives, reporters, cops, neighbors. Phones ringing with condolences, leads, questions, more condolences. There was paperwork and copies of paperwork and copies of copied paperwork. There were pontifications and likelihoods and theories (Halloween-occult kidnapping, child slave trade, and the most sickening: me and my wife, Vivian, were behind it). There were facts and almost-facts—a neighbor said the car that carried her off was a gray Subaru; a woman thought she saw Ella in an Albany Walmart. But all of this led only to cars that looked like the Subaru seen speeding down the road that morning, to a girl who looked a little something like Ella. Not to the car that took her, not to Ella herself. And so our lives sprawled toward the accumulating evidence of the human life we sought but never to the actual life itself; we were at once contracted, compressed into a diminutive, unlivable space, one without our daughter.

Now my mind slips into a recurring alcoholic fantasy in which I find the man that took her and hunt him down, sometimes in an ordinary neighborhood where he has hidden Ella in his perfectly normal two-story house, sometimes in a shanty cabin hidden in the thick woods, sometimes, and this is on my darkest days, in a crude hole dug out in a forest where he has forced her to hide out. There are various versions of the finding. But there are no alternate endings. I always find her, and I always carry her back home in my arms.

As I slip into a watery cave of sleep I wonder, why not a fantasy that prevents the taking in the first place? Why this way?

I WAKE up on the next morning crumpled in my chair. I unpack myself painfully and stretch my neck in what feels like an impossible direction. A headache spring-releases itself and I fall, nearly forward, out of the chair, righting myself with massive effort and heading heavily toward the stairs. The sun is just coming up; in thirty minutes both kids will be awake, demanding breakfast. I stumble through our dark bedroom and into the bathroom where I stop, surprised, but then again not surprised, to see Vivian still in the tub.

She is awake. Probably has been all night.

"I slept in here so I would miss my alarm," she offers, like a practical confession.

I massage the back of my neck. "Why would you want to miss your alarm?"

"So that I wouldn't get Ella up in time, and she'd miss the bus, and I'd let her play hooky so we could hang out all day."

I stare into her pallid face. This is not the face of delusion, or confusion, but of causal reasoning. *Magical thinking,* as we learned in therapy, the belief that one's thoughts can change the narrative of events. That one could relive the event and change it, such as by sleeping in the bathtub and missing an alarm, therefore altering a sequence of events that have already occurred.

"Will you turn the water on?" she asks.

"While you're in your clothes?"

She nods.

I stare at her, limp in the tub as if she is paralyzed. It seems a simple request, though strange, and I don't want to deny her.

I turn on the faucet, adjusting hot and cold until it feels right. I stand there for a minute, watching the water run. I don't know what I'm doing, running the water on my wife with her clothes on. I have nothing to offer her. Somewhere I stopped persisting. I've failed her as a husband, as a father.

Water starts to form a little pool underneath her. It's taking forever. It will take forever to fill this bathtub, it seems. This bathtub is a trench. A deep trench. It will hold, once it's filled, the body of water that separates us, a trench as deep and as wide as our missing daughter.

Once, when Vivian first started diving, she was nervous and unskilled, and she breathed her air down below five hundred pounds. I was ten feet away, watching a school of grunts, when she signaled me, panicked, her fist closed and hitting the center of her chest, the diver's signal for *low on air*. I swam to her, and she grabbed my safe second regulator, replacing her own regulator in her mouth, and we traveled carefully together to the top.

On the surface, she clung to me, perfectly still in the water, while we waited for the other divers to ascend. On the boat back to the resort, she sat with her entire body pushed up against the side of me, both hands wrapped around my forearm, her grip never letting up. I was positive that fear had destroyed her scuba career, and this would be her last dive. But when she returned to the water two days later, she dove without hesitation, as if she needed the sea to have its way with her, to search and turn her out, to be enemy first, before it could become friend.

The water in the tub inches up, passing halfway. She sinks down to meet it, water up to her mouth. *This has gone on too long now*, I think, turning toward the faucet.

"Please," she says softly. "Please just let me go down and not ever come up."

I pause over this clothed woman in a bathtub, who is essentially begging for death. My wife, who has been vanishing for years. The fantasy in which I bring my daughter home goes exactly that way because I know, from a place of tortured understanding that I can't ever not lose her. It can never un-happen. But maybe, maybe she can be returned. And I find myself kneeling by the tub as the water rises. Maybe she can be returned, I think. I place both hands on Vivian's chest. Maybe she should be returned to the water. Slowly I push her down into the water until she is completely submerged. She's calm. It's as if she has been waiting for this: clean, justified relief. I hold her firmly under as she blinks at me, eyes wide and sad and willing, little bubbles floating up from her mouth. After many seconds she puts her hands on my forearms, the way she did on the boat, and squeezes. I wait. She merely grips, the rest of her body still. *How long*, I think. *How long until this is over*. I feel her grip tighten and then start to tug. Her eyes narrow a bit, focusing. She tugs harder, then pushes against my arms, trying to move them. I secure my position, bracing myself against the side of the tub for what will come next. She tugs for a few more seconds. Then it comes. Legs kicking in the water, her body frantically writhing. Her head tosses this way and that, her fingernails claw at my arms, water comes over the tub, water is going everywhere.

Her entire body is in the throes of a full-throttle thrash. The force is surprising. I have to put my entire weight on her to keep her down. She's putting up a wild fight. But I persist. Her lungs must be pure fire. She's really fighting me now. But I persist. I persist for another second, then another, then another. Then one more and I release her, and she comes out of the water like some dripping, magnificent creature—like that first time I saw her on the beach with her friends, and she regarded me with shy suspicion, and I followed her. I wouldn't stop following her until she resigned herself to me, until she gave herself over to the truth that I would give her the air out of my lungs if she needed it, that I would always pull her to the surface no matter how long it took to get there, or how far up we had to go, or how much she begged me to keep her under. I would always pull her up even if there was nothing worth living for up here. Nothing except the two of us in the world, losing and finding and sharing our breath in the bottomless waterway of dark, terrible things.

GUEST ROOM
GUEST ROOM

After the incident, Corinne sat alone in the guest room and tried to recall what exactly had happened. A hand under her shirt while she slept in the guest room after feeling sick at a friend's party, that hand under the bra that had been unhooked, a hand traveling down, or back up from that place. Whatever the direction, Corinne couldn't exactly say. She had woken up in the middle of it, or at the end of it, realizing the hand and the face peering at her in the dark belonged not to her husband, Ben. Not to her husband, but to his brother Lucas. Then Ben finding her wild and awake, asking what's wrong, her vague account, his dash from the room to find his brother, the confrontation in the living room, the spectating party guests, Ben's hands around his brother's throat. Then the denial by Lucas, so adamant that for a small second Corinne felt she'd made a dark mistake.

That she couldn't say exactly what had happened made the idea of calling the police a brief and impossible thought. That it was a family affair complicated the matter even more. She and Ben had only just arrived at twenty-three. The marriage was not even three years old. Too young and too ill-equipped to handle such abnormality, such confusion and uncertainty. She and Ben simply returned home after the incident, shocked and exhausted. Ben suggested there was nothing to do but remove the relationship with Lucas from their lives. That was reasonable justice. A domestic punishment fitting and fair, editing him out of the family like a scene in a movie. After that, the incident was no longer discussed, as that only seemed to pay homage to the aberrancy.

JUST over a year later in early fall, a female detective called. She was inquiring about the whereabouts of Lucas, who was missing and wanted for a sexual crime against another woman. Corinne pressed the phone tightly against her ear, afraid she'd made a mistake. Her brother-in-law was not removed but lurking off set, going bad in the wings. She found herself explaining the event at the party to the detective, surprised at how an entire year of silence could unspool instantly through one single word, a word she had never used before, the word *assault*.

"Actually it's not assault," the detective countered, "unless you can say there was penetration. In the state of New Jersey, sexual assault is the legal term for rape. Plus, you're beyond the statute of limitations for reporting the crime. If you had called the police we could have booked him on lewd and lascivious behavior."

Lewd and lascivious behavior, Corinne repeated to herself as she hung up the phone, a wild numbness taking over. *That has such a nice ring to it.*

Or, rather, that *had* a nice ring to it. In the weeks following, she couldn't stop thinking about the statute of limitations, as if the crime had ended and was not even hers anymore. The crime that once had a name but no longer.

She felt estranged from her own private encounters, and that estrangement began to strangle her days with Ben, the man she married fast, somewhat impulsively, because she'd always possessed an urgency around marriage and he seemed a good man. And he *was* good—he was the man who had left the guest room to go after his brother. A valiant response, Corinne tried to remind herself. What any woman would want, for her husband to try to kill the bastard, because an event was nothing until a man got physical about it. But was the rise of the adrenaline necessary to prove the violence of the crime true? Was this somehow all about Ben and his reaction?

"Why did you leave me so fast that night?" she asked, after being seated at their favorite steak place, one Friday evening in late September. She'd asked for a seat near the window, to watch the last of the leaves fall.

Ben blinked slowly, as if trying to locate *that night.* Then he shook his head. "I wanted to break his neck. I was angry. I was enraged at what he did to you."

So many *I*s, she thought. "You *were* angry?"

"It's been a year, Cor. Why are we even talking about this? You're fine. Right?"

She stared at him, hoping he would take back what he just said, that he would see that something was happening in her, that a void was opening or had already opened, that she was an empty room behind a closed door, and he needed to go in and sit there with her the way he had not the first time, for as long as she needed.

"We should take a vacation," Ben said, as if *that night* was gone, over, no longer something to bother them.

In the next few weeks, she found herself withdrawing. She spoke less and less to Ben. It wasn't purposeful—this silent treatment—she was just emptied and swept out of things to say. What did it matter, saying things out loud? Every word was in danger of being left alone long enough to expire. They were two actors on the same stage, reading different scripts. His called *Why Are We Even Talking About This?* She felt she needed time alone, apart from him. He was frustrated and angry, but mostly irritated about being disrupted. She offered to move out but he said he'd rent an apartment across town, which surprised her, until she recognized that his leaving was in no way an unfamiliar move on his part.

She stayed in the house and kept her days busy working as an admin in a real-estate firm. But at night, the house towered in its emptiness. She found it hard to sleep. She was afraid to be alone.

After the first of the year, she called her friend Gayle, an older divorcée who had received a lot of money in the divorce settlement. Now that Gayle was single, she was always at the bar, dressed smartly in black, expensive fabrics like silk and suede. She was looking for a partner in crime, as she called it. Corinne met her one evening for drinks.

"You mean, just separated? Why? Did something happen?" Gayle asked.

Lewd and lascivious behavior, Corinne wanted to say. Although she had never reported it, which meant she couldn't call it that. Which meant technically it had never happened.

"Maybe we got married too fast," Corinne said.

"That can be a problem." Gayle shrugged. "How is it living alone?"

"Terrifying. Are you afraid of being alone at night in your house?"

"Me? Oh no, honey. I lived with his noise for twenty years. I wrap myself up in all that quiet!"

Corinne tried to wrap herself up in all that quiet. But the tree branch knocking against the window was someone tapping on it. Car headlights swept through her kitchen like flashlights. The wind whispered like vandals conversing in the living room. She forced herself to lie in her empty bed at night and pull terror up to her chin like a blanket. It was a meditative journey, she decided. A hard investment in the soul. She would go into the terror and return with more of herself.

But she was too distracted for soul investments. Distracted but still hollow. She started on an early spring reading list of novels, letting language fill in the blank pages of her mind. But the sentences slid around, bumping into each other one after another, yielding no comprehension. Words seemed independent from—even indifferent to—each other.

She tried magazines and newspapers—short, digestible, pulpy material. But it was the same result. She stumbled onto the crossword in the Sunday paper. That famous puzzle, its black and white rows and columns intersecting quietly, waiting to be answered. Maybe, Corinne thought, she had been approaching her emptiness the wrong way. Maybe it was she who had to return the words to the blank page.

But two hours later she only had *IRS*, the three-letter word for tax org. Seven-letter word for *childhood disease*? Not *Rocky Mountain spotted fever*, not *chicken pox*. *Rubella* would have worked had it not intersected vertically with the *S* in *IRS*. One correct answer had only invalidated another.

Frustrated, she checked the answer key. Seven-letter word for *childhood disease* was *measles*. Of course! How could she miss *measles*? *Rubella* was close, but this wasn't about close. It was about exactly right. And consulting the key made Corinne feel like a cheat, a failure. She thought it profoundly unreasonable that the crossword required such impossible precision.

She bought a big book of crosswords divided up into levels: easy, medium, and diabolical. The plan was to start on *easy* and not move on until each puzzle was solved. She would work her way up, relearn what to call things, train herself to become an ambassador of semantic precision.

"I don't know what anything is called precisely," Corinne told Gayle at the bar. She had been on the first puzzle in *easy* for three weeks and it was still mostly blank. She was exhausted.

"What are you talking about?"

"Crosswords. I can't solve them!"

"Don't worry, I'm no good either. Although I haven't done one in years."

"Five-letter word for *Bert's friend*," Corinne said. "What *is* that?"

"Really?" Gayle said, sounding a little shocked. "It's Ernie. That's an easy one."

Ernie. Of course. Corinne was embarrassed and then indignant. She had thought of every famous Bert she knew, which, as it turned out, was only one: Burt Reynolds. Now she remembered that Burt Reynolds wasn't even spelled with an *E*. What in the world was she thinking?

Five-letter word for Bert's friend, she said to herself on the ride home. *Ernie. Bert and Ernie. Ten-letter word for* Lewd's friend. *Lascivious. Lewd and Lascivious.*

Before the call from the detective, Corinne would have had no problem recalling the names *Bert* and *Ernie*, but now it appeared she was beyond the statute of limitations for naming.

Just before Easter, Corinne received a call from Ben.

"How are you?" he asked.

"It's official," she said. "I'm no ambassador."

"What do you mean?"

"I don't even know. That's the problem."

Ben paused. "Do you want me to come home?"

She imagined him coming home. He was a good man, she thought. But incapable of handling her wordlessness. And in the vision of his return home she saw herself resigning to the guest room of her own life, always an outsider, always alone.

"I just don't know," she answered.

Corinne and Gayle started meeting at the martini bar two or three times a week. Corinne was consuming a lot of martinis. She ordered extra-dirty martinis, shaken not stirred, with extra olives. The longest and most specific drink she could order. She discovered that martinis dampened the terror at home. She could fall into a watery sleep and not imagine that the lock on the front door was being fiddled with.

She also noticed a new feeling when she drank, like a car peeling off in her chest, leaving tracks of burning rubber around her heart.

"Do you ever feel a burning in your chest?" she asked Gayle.

"Around your heart? No, but it's quite common."

"It is? What would you call that?"

"Heartburn," Gayle said, definitively. "Take an antacid."

Corinne stopped at the drugstore on the way home and picked up a plastic tub of antacids. She popped one before martinis, one after. Cherry-flavored circles of chalk that changed nothing. In fact, she started to feel pain when she ate. A bite of an apple, a forkful of salad, and she felt gassy, bloated.

"It's probably an ulcer," Gayle told her over martinis. "You're so young. You should go to the doctor."

Corinne went to the doctor, a baby-faced twenty-something who didn't look old enough to have finished medical school.

"It's an ulcer," he said emphatically.

"Are you positive?"

"Yes. But we should give you an endoscopy to rule out anything else."

"*Anything else* like what?"

"Stomach cancer."

"Do *you* think I have stomach cancer?"

"No, but we should just be sure."

The procedure was two thousand dollars. Corinne didn't understand the point in spending two thousand dollars for the doctor to say "It's an ulcer" when he had already said it for free. She returned home with a prescription for a stronger antacid and *no more alcohol*, doctor's orders.

No more martinis with Gayle in the bar. Corinne's evenings became vacant and dry. She longed to say the words *extra-dirty martini, shaken not stirred, with extra olives*. The creaks in the house went back to being the team of thieves lowering themselves from the roof into the windows.

She felt she needed a sober activity out of the house that would eat up her time. She decided to try bingo. The only game around was in a bad part of town in the old gymnasium of a now-defunct school. She was younger than everyone by at least fifty years. But there was a game every night. And there was something about people yelling *Bingo!* There was no mistake what *Bingo!* meant. It meant somebody won, and now it was time for a new game. It was specific and epiphanic. Like saying *I figured it out!* or *That's exactly right!* No other words needed.

Corinne arrived home one evening after bingo and stopped in the doorway. All the lights in the house were on. A chair in the kitchen had been turned on its side. The drawers of her vanity had been rummaged through.

Her fear was happening. She had been vandalized.

"I will need a list of the missing items," the cop told her after he arrived and was filling out the report.

Corinne hesitated. "I'm not sure they took anything."

"But there was a break-in?"

"Yes. Things were out of place. Lights on. Drawers rifled through."

"But nothing is missing?"

"Maybe something is missing. I just haven't found it yet."

"Do you know the point of entry?"

Corinne looked around. "The front door?"

"Was the door unlocked?"

She shook her head.

"Was the lock broken or the door kicked in?"

"No. Maybe they came through a window?"

"Is there a window broken out anywhere?"

She shook her head again, realizing that the cop's forehead had furrowed itself into a crinkled mess, as if he didn't believe her.

"Maybe through the attic?" she suggested.

The cop scratched his head and sighed. "Ma'am, are you sure you didn't leave those lights on and just don't remember? And maybe you went through those drawers looking for something?"

He thought she was crazy, she knew it. The leading actress in the latest straight-to-DVD movie, *Robbed of a Robbery*. Her chest burned.

"I'm sure."

The cop finished the report and left. In the days after, Corinne found she was afraid to leave the house for long periods of time because it meant she might return to a possible break-in. She called in sick to work. "I have an ulcer," she said. Even though her chest felt raw, grated upon, she liked the way her words sounded. It was an extra-dirty martini, shaken not stirred, with extra olives. A small cure for her vagueness.

After calling in sick for several days, Corinne finally took a medical leave of absence. She tooled around the house in her robe for two weeks. While flowers bloomed outside, she divided her time between looking up alternative cures for ulcers on the Internet and checking all the locks.

Aloe vera juice, licorice extract, chamomile tea.

Front door, side door, back door, check.

She tracked her ulcer as if it were the weather. Monday, a high around the heart, with each breath at a ninety percent chance of feeling like it's being restricted by a steel plate in the chest. Wednesday, dull pain under the rib cage, with a sixty percent chance of the pain becoming hot and sharp by the end of the day.

GAYLE called Corinne one evening in late May and invited her over for tea. Corinne was not sure what surprised her more—the invite or the fact that Gayle was drinking tea. Corinne agreed to leave her house for one hour.

Gayle lived in an upscale loft with distressed hardwood floors and an oversized balcony. The whole place was decorated in lavender and teal, colors that Gayle's ex-husband hated. But now Gayle was completely untethered. Divorce fit her perfectly. Corinne wondered if she could be a divorced woman. She and Ben had been separated for almost five months. But trying on the thought of freedom seemed cruel. Ben had not been unkind to her; he had only unknowingly confirmed how alone she was in the world.

Gayle had purchased the same book of crossword puzzles. Corinne picked it up from the side table and flipped through it. The book was filled with answers, even a few in diabolical.

"What is this?" Corinne held it up as if she had discovered some incriminating piece of evidence.

"I started doing crosswords too," Gayle said, smiling. "Martinis got old. I'm hooked!"

"You said you were no good at them!"

"Thought I'd try my hand at it again. Turns out I'm not bad."

Corinne felt betrayed. Crosswords had been Corinne's hobby, or at least, her failed hobby. Even that was no longer hers. Gayle was a woman who had left her husband in a fit of boredom and then taken him for everything in the settlement. Gayle relished the quiet because nothing had been stolen from her in the dead of night. She had not been robbed of her ability to know what happened and call things what they were. She was fat and happy with all the things she still possessed.

Gayle sat down on the couch and kicked her feet up under her. "I'm really stuck on one that's bothering me. Four-letter word for kinship, real or perceived."

Corinne's chest was so enflamed that her neck felt like it was on fire. She needed to get home before she was robbed.

"That's easy," she said. "Lewd."

CORINNE stopped taking Gayle's calls after their visit. She had no business cavorting with a happy divorcée who was a master at crosswords. Gayle was diabolical, Corinne decided. A diabolical crossword thief.

Corinne went back to work, no longer tracking the pain because it was everywhere, all the time. A permanent houseguest in her body. Not her friendly ulcer but a deep gnawing, like a raccoon in her stomach, always chewing. She hardly ate. By summer she had lost fifteen pounds and started to look gaunt, like a cancer patient. She went back to the doctor.

"The ulcer might be bleeding," he told her. "But I suspect it's something more serious. You really need to get the scope."

Two weeks later, Corinne got the scope. Then she went home and crawled into bed.

She dreamed that she came home to her house, completely empty. Everything gone. When the police came and asked her for a list of missing things, she blanked. She couldn't for the life of her remember the name of that box that played movies. The word for the rectangular sleeping cushion escaped her. Who could say what you call that round wooden object with things for sitting in the kitchen.

Corinne woke up to a noise in the house. She grabbed the baseball bat from the closet and inched her way into the living room, ready to swing. It was dark, quiet. She turned on the light. Everything seemed in place except the keyboard on her desk was upside down and a few papers had been thrown on the floor. Had someone popped in just to mess up her desk? Was she going crazy? Is that what you called this?

The doctor called her into his office a few days later. He looked serious, enigmatic.

"We didn't find anything," the doctor told her.

"You didn't find any cancer?"

"We didn't find *anything*," the doctor repeated. "Not even an ulcer."

"What?" Corinne felt dizzy. "You were positive it was an ulcer!"

"Only the scope can confirm that. You just have a sensitive stomach, prone to being agitated. This is good news. You should be relieved."

Corinne got out of there as fast as she could. She knew she should feel relieved, but she wasn't. The ulcer gave her something to go on. It was a real medical fact. A named entity, printed in a textbook somewhere with symptoms, diagnosis, prognosis. Now there was nothing to point to except *prone to being agitated*. Nothing but an inclination. A predisposition. A nameless void.

She felt monumentally misguided. Disillusioned. She felt entitled, at the very least, to an ulcer.

She didn't want to go home. She was afraid of home, that big empty place where all of her things were, those things that were always almost getting robbed. She could just keep driving, she thought. She would start over somewhere else. Get a small place with deadbolts and a bat. She would get a gun. She would divorce Ben, nice Ben, but nevertheless the Ben who peered into the nothingness inside her, the Ben who looked so much like his brother.

Instead Corinne went to the bar, where she ordered an extra-dirty martini, shaken not stirred, with extra olives. Where she also ran into Gayle.

"What happened to you?" Gayle asked.

"I've been working."

"Oh. You haven't returned my calls. Do you like my new color?" Gayle smoothed her hand over her hair. "It's called *best-dressed burgundy*."

Best-dressed burgundy. There were names for hair colors, names for martinis, names for crimes that hadn't actually been committed. But there was not a name for what was happening in her marriage. There was not a name for what was happening in her body.

"There's something you may want to know," Gayle said, her eyes darkening. "I heard that Ben's seeing another woman."

Corinne swirled the extra olives around in her martini. She was moved—how could the news not move her—but she was not surprised. She hadn't spoken to him in months. She had stopped taking his calls. He was performing his sequel, *Forget Normalcy and Just Move On.*

"Hello?" Gayle waved her hand in front of Corinne's face. "What are you going to do about this?"

"Nothing," Corinne said.

The pain in her stomach was starting up again. That horrible gnawing, that rabid raccoon, that *Dear God just what was that thing in her body?* Her body, with all those dials and gauges measuring the unknown, that dark basement of shame and startling emptiness, a place where there was memory but no recollection, where there was pain but no ulcer?

Corinne went home after the bar closed and walked right in on a man in the living room standing by the coffee table, dressed in a black T-shirt and a ski mask not pulled over his face. Had she not been so stupefied to see an actual thief in her house, she would have been terrified.

"What are you doing?" she asked him.

The man—he was not a man but just a young boy. A teenager. He looked caught.

"Are you the one who's been breaking in?" she asked.

The boy nodded. His arms hung down at his sides. He had nothing in his hands—no flashlight or bag. He was dressed as a burglar but did not appear to be burgling, just standing there.

"Why don't you ever take anything? Why are you messing with me?"

The boy swallowed as if afraid to speak.

"Well? You're standing in my house. I deserve an answer."

"I just liked the feeling," he said, not looking at her.

"The feeling of what?"

"Of being where I'm not supposed to. I didn't mean anything by it."

"You didn't mean anything by it?" Corinne wanted to throw a chair at his head. She wanted to wrestle him to the ground. "The police think I'm nuts. *I* think I'm nuts. You're like a ghost, moving this or that, making me crazy."

"I'm sorry." Just like that he started to cry.

She watched him, a budding young star in this year's breakthrough drama, *A Sniveling Thief. This is getting out of control*, she thought.

"OK," she said, finally. "This is what we're going to do. You're going to rob me."

His crying came to a sniffled stop. She stood there, staring through him.

"What?" he asked.

"That's right. If you're going to break into my house, you're going to finish the job. You're going to rob me. You're going to take some very specific things, some things that I can name to the police for a police report."

"You're asking me to rip you off?"

"Bingo!" Corinne felt maniacal and alive. "Don't worry. I'm not going to turn you in."

The kid was hunched over now. He looked pathetic. This was obviously more than he had bargained for.

Corinne went into the kitchen and returned with a garbage bag.

"Listen to me," she said. "I have some jewelry that's been passed down from the women in my family. You will take that. Some china, given to me at my wedding, that's worth more than your life. I don't want anyone saying that this robbery was in vain."

Corinne followed the kid around while he filled the bag. The china, the jewelry, a picture of Corinne and her father that he gave her just before he died. A stuffed bear she'd had since childhood. The breakable items clinked about inside the bag. Occasionally the kid would glance at Corinne, with a look that begged for his release. *You're not going anywhere,* her look said back to him.

When his bag was full, she walked him to the door.

"Now, I'll give you fifteen minutes before I call the police. You live around here?"

The kid nodded.

"Good, that will give you time to get home, get inside, and stash the stuff. Don't tell anyone. That's a rookie mistake! The only way to keep a secret between two people is if both of them are dead. That might be a good thing to remember if you choose to pursue a life of crime."

She watched as he trudged down the street with the trash bag. The bag swayed this way and that, clanking and banging, as if it were waving at her, as if it were saying goodbye.

When Corinne could no longer see the trash bag, she felt a sad completion in knowing exactly what had been taken from her. The heirloom of femininity, a beautiful but breakable token of marriage, the snapshot of a vigilant memory, the remains of childhood innocence. Precious and irreplaceable things. Things that the thief would toss aside in his room, never understanding the value of what he had taken, understanding even less the cost of what he had left behind.

You Play Me, I'll Play Lulu

I am sitting out on my balcony with the contents of my sister Lulu's box. It's an early summer Texas evening, and I am vividly remembering a different summer evening, ten years earlier, when Lulu was introduced to mushrooms, suffused by an endless rotation of the Grateful Dead on the record player. Lulu was just out of high school and had this boyfriend—one of those artificially constructed hippies of the '90s who marched against yuppies and forsook all instruments of personal hygiene. He was one boyfriend in a string of boyfriends who wrapped themselves around her life. They looked deep into each other's eyes with transient longing; they wrestled in slow motion on the floor while their fingers and toes intertwined, phalange poetry. *We're transcending,* they told each other. I feigned fifteen-year-old disinterest but secretly spied on them, mystified and curious, as they mistook angst for enlightenment, serotonin reactors for spirituality. I didn't know what I was seeing. I couldn't possibly imagine what the dead would be grateful for. And my sister was an agonizing and beautiful dance I didn't understand. A dance I never thought would end. But it would. Not because Jerry Garcia would be dead in two years but because my sister would be dead in one.

Two weeks ago I visited my older sister Gigi in Manhattan. I hadn't seen her since our mother's funeral, three years earlier. Turns out, Gigi has quite the life. She's in advertising, and she's some burgeoning big shot, and there's a martini bar on the bottom floor of her obscenely priced apartment building. The night I arrived, we bellied up to the bar where I observed socialites with bored eyes and smug mouths that I guessed were symptomatic of raging self-importance.

Gigi was dressed in all black. Though she's two years older than I am she looked younger and not related to me—lean, with a sinewy beauty and black hair that fell straight down to the center of her back. Her thing was dirty martinis and deadpanning. Apparently, the only way to fly these days in NYC.

"You look good," she told me, eyeing my long straggly hair and thrift-store bellbottoms.

"I've gained fifteen pounds."

"OK, you look like hell. Have they been hog-tying you out there in the Old West? Is that a real thing, hog-tying?"

I shrugged.

"What have you been doing?" she asked incriminatingly. I felt the sudden need for an alibi.

"I'm the office administrator at the community college."

"That's still happening? I thought you were writing a book."

"I'm working on it," I said.

She nodded and didn't say anything else. This felt like false neutrality. I imagined she was thinking all sorts of things she would never ever say.

The next day, she took me to her office and introduced me to fashionable, upwardly-mobile coworkers as her sister, Cici, and it wasn't until we got into her office—an oversized version of a movie-set office—that I realized she was a little put-off. I figured my presence was ruining the gig a bit. Gigi is the kind of name that works as a solo act. Couple it with Cici and suddenly we're a singing comedy duo. If Lulu had been there, well, we would have been a pack of strippers.

If Lulu had been there. That fragment of a thought drifted past my eyes like a veil of smoke, then disappeared.

Back at Gigi's place she had all sorts of expensive art and furniture and decorative pieces that I've only seen in magazines. The contrast between her meticulous, modern flat and my empty, dull apartment was startling. Stacking our lives up against each other, one would find nothing to connect us in any way, nothing except for the hidden past, the murky lake of shared history.

My eye caught a glimpse of a strange object on Gigi's sofa-back table, an incense stick, dropped into some kind of blown-glass art bowl that probably cost more than my car. The earthy relic seemed like an accident in such an aseptic abode, nostalgic evidence of our sister Lulu, left behind like a piece of DNA passed over in the wiping down of the past.

I almost mentioned it but decided not to. I wouldn't be able to stand that look of non-recognition on Gigi's face, the one that's adjusted to the dim light of erasure, the one that looks so much like our sister I would have to look away.

I AM sitting out on the balcony with the contents of the box that lived in the attic of my mother's house before she died from alcoholism. It was the house in which we had grown up, a place where Gigi and I were bad girls asking for bad things to happen. Built sometime in the eighteenth century, the house had two sets of stairs, and when Gigi and I snuck out of the house to meet boys, we used the stairs that ran down into the kitchen. One evening we snuck down those steps to find Lulu sitting at the kitchen table. She was two weeks from graduating. She'd had it so easy—prom queen, student council president, valedictorian. So popular that she'd even had her own stalker, a freshman girl who'd lopped off a chunk of Lulu's hair with a pair of scissors. But Lulu had even handled this with ease, covering up the mishap with a shoulder-length bob that became the rage among her classmates, and never speaking of the event again. Gigi was jealous of her, which meant, by extension, I was too, if I wanted any protection. But secretly I admired her:

that long graceful neck, the way she watched herself brush her hair in the mirror, one perfectly reflected stroke after another.

Lulu raised a single eyebrow at us. "What are you doing?"

"Meeting boys," Gigi answered.

"Are you aware that you look ridiculous?"

I sized up seventeen-year-old Gigi. Between her halter-top and my red lipstick I felt we had aged ourselves at least a year. The kind of sophistication that warranted use of our full first names: Regina and Cecelia.

"The boys don't think so," Gigi snapped.

"Yes they do. That's why they're into you. You look ridiculously easy."

Gigi crossed her arms defiantly and took a small step out in front of me. It was her way of putting a physical block between us—me and Gigi on one side of the barrier, Lulu on the other.

"We think we look good."

"Clearly that's the problem."

Lulu had that face on, that face that was smiling with no smile. Gigi hated this face. The deep resonance in Lulu's eyes, the silent harmonics we could never address. Lulu had won before we even knew we were in a fight.

"Do you know what percentage of women under eighteen get attacked? You're asking for it."

"We *get* it," Gigi said. "You're better than everyone. You're going to live forever in your high, lonely tower, *Leslie Gray Martin*." Using Lulu's full name was a way for Gigi to strike hard and deeply at Lulu. "Lulu" had been a self-assigned nickname—an exotic rebranding. Gigi was reminding her of the ordinary girl underneath.

Gigi stormed out and I followed. I had no choice, really. But at the door, I turned and caught Lulu's profile. She was turned enough toward me that I could see her face had dropped, and her eyelids had lowered like a heavy curtain, a wash of dread coming down.

Then she glanced up at me, and already, the look was gone. So fast I wondered if I had even seen it.

THE day I was scheduled to leave Manhattan, Gigi had a morning meeting at the office she couldn't miss. The visit had been mostly uneventful, no notable sibling bonding. Gigi won't go there; it's not her way. For her, the visit was strictly a matter of older sister due diligence—checking my vitals in person, logging a little face time. This was fine with me. I didn't need to walk away with any fortified sisterly bonding or newfound clarity. I just needed to walk away with the box.

Gigi told me that when she sold our mother's house, she got rid of everything. The way she said the word *everything,* as if to put a cover over the event, only unveiled that it was a lie: she had not gotten rid of everything. She had not gotten rid of the box. The box my mother had kept hidden away in the attic. The few remaining items of Lulu.

Gigi wanted these things, but she didn't need them. Not like I needed them. After Gigi left for work I didn't have much time until the cab arrived, so I went straight into her bedroom and stood before her things—a piece of framed art, a black platform bed, a nightstand, a glass bookcase, a single black mahogany dresser. In the closet her clothes hung in varying strips of black fabrics. But in this bare, urban coffin of a room I found no box.

I checked all the other places in her flat that might be hiding a medium-sized moving box: bathroom closet, hall closet, guest bedroom closet. Nothing. Kitchen pantry, utility room, balcony storage. Still nothing. I had to find it. I would not be coming back here for another trip.

After searching the entire place, I wound up back in the living room by the glass bowl with the incense. One touch with my finger, and the end of it crumbled instantly to dust. The incense was old. Very, very old. It had come here, I realized, in a box. A box that was no longer here but left a trace.

I AM sitting out on the balcony with the contents of the box, rescued by me from Gigi who rescued it from my mother's house after she died from alcoholism, although this is a misnomer. One doesn't die from alcoholism, one dies from the effects of alcohol: brain aneurysm, cirrhosis of the liver, or choking on one's vomit, which is how my mother went. Even victims in horror films exit more gracefully than my mother did. So I grant her some poetry by saying she died from alcoholism, as in, she died of sadness, abject loneliness, a broken heart. Because what had become the residual, dark stone on her life was that morning in the kitchen where we waited at the table for Lulu, who was not coming down, my mother calling and calling, her fury rising as the eggs turned cold.

So it was most likely out of her guilt, rather than remembrance, that she kept the box. After all, my mother believed that left-behind objects had the power to turn us phantom simply by trapping us in the past through our looking at them. She had gotten rid of the rest of Lulu's things after her death, just like she had destroyed all pictures of our father.

Gigi and I used to ask my mother what our father looked like, having been too young to remember when he left. She would always answer with things like, "Oh, he had one of those mouths with the lips and those hands with the fingers." When she did not feel like playing the game she would say, "He looked like what someone walking away looks like." My mother's melancholia was not to be touched, so Gigi and I would ask no more questions but instead try to picture what someone always walking away would look like—a back of a head of hair, the concavity of a knee closing and opening, the sole of one shoe, the sole of the other. In our minds our father was merely a collection of abstract, scrambled parts, always faceless. Real but veiled. Something to which we found ourselves attributing our existence but not our essence. Because our father possessed no essence. He was cold biology. That he was our father was just a fact, true but innocuous, the belief in another galaxy that we would never see.

Lulu never participated in the line of questioning about our father. She remained hard and silent in her disinterest about such things. In this way, I imagine, she actually remained close to our father. She held on to some visage of him, anchored herself in some memory, made true through her persistence in holding onto it. This is what weighed on her, that he was not a faraway object on which to gaze, a dim star. He may have been without her, but she was not without him. He was somewhere much closer in the world, much too close, and carrying on, roaming the earth with all the authority of a creator.

My mother sent me that morning to bring Lulu down after calling her for too long. But the door was closed, and the knock returned no answer, and so I turned away and went back downstairs.

The balcony on which I sit with the contents of Lulu's box is in a place far away from Gigi and her pop-up book of skyscrapers. It's the balcony of a one-bedroom apartment in the Old West, where they may or may not hog-tie. I came to Texas on an undergraduate scholarship, a move that disguised itself as a pilgrimage away from all that had clogged my soul, but over time it turned back into what it was, which was just my life, moved down and to the left. I return to all the things I have not accomplished or achieved. This non-achievement is worse for me because I was supposed to achieve great things after I published a novella my junior year in high school, after being called a "teenaged wonder" and someone to "watch out for" in *Seventeen Magazine.* But here I am, eight years later, allegedly working on a novel. Truthfully, there is no one to be watched out for here. Out here it's the dead of summer, a wasteland where I've thrown myself away. A container of empty days in which I've been sealed.

From my balcony I have visuals on four fast-food places, a thrift store and three more apartment complexes, all on the other side of the noisy, traffic-jammed highway that cuts in front of my place. Urban sprawl is lifeless, urban sprawl is terrible, urban sprawl should be killing me. Instead I find it comforting. It reflects nothing but objects that are concrete and decentralized. All I have left of Lulu are objects, also concrete and decentralized.

And sometimes from this balcony I imagine someone else in a similar balcony across the highway looking back at me, a mirror, and I must retreat back inside.

AFTER I had touched the incense between my fingers, I returned to Gigi's room. At the foot of the bed I put my hand on the burgundy duvet and walked the length of it while running my fingertips over the cold cotton. At the pillows, the duvet had been neatly folded down to reveal a burgundy silk sheet. I touched the sheet; it felt thick, as if there was something underneath. Pulling it back, I discovered a thin, patchwork quilt laid neatly underneath it. A quilt that was not Gigi's.

I approached the bookshelf where hardcovers and paperbacks and big art books lined up end to end, shelf after shelf. I ran my hand along the book tops on the shelf at my eye level, stopping at one book with a missing binding and tilting it out toward me with one finger, as if this was a trigger that might open a secret door somewhere. A book of poetry, one that did not belong to Gigi, just like the quilt. There were two others I detected as I scanned the rest of the bookcase. Books, quilt, incense. All things that came here in a box. Almost all, I thought, as I glanced at the framed piece of art on the wall.

My cab was due in ten minutes. I worked quickly, unhooking the frame from the wall and removing the rigid backboard to discover, taped to the back of the art print, an old poster with crumbling edges.

I left the city, my suitcase a little heavier than it had been when I arrived. My visit with Gigi had not been to verify the existence of my only living sibling but to verify that trace of the blood that no longer remains.

BEYOND the balcony where I sit with the contents of the box, the sun is beginning to set. It's that time when the day pulls twilight down like a dark shade over the sky, and in turn, twilight will pull down the darker curtain of dusk.

Sometimes when I think about Lulu, I try to imagine when it happened exactly. To organize the event into a singular point of time, a crystallized moment, unambiguous and compact. Something I can put in my hand and close my fist around.

My mother had gone to work early that evening to work the night shift. Gigi, graduated and bored, and me, just bored, made a gas station run for some snacks. We ended up idling, flipping through trashy magazines, perusing the candy aisle. Then took a drive and shared some cigarettes. It was dark when we returned, and it didn't occur to us to check on Lulu. Nineteen-year-old Lulu hiding out in the house instead of spreading her wings against the sky of adulthood. Going nowhere, withdrawing more, vanishing harder.

Did she find the rich violence of that moment beautifully and cheaply juxtaposed against the fact that her sisters were idling around in a dirty gas station? Had we checked on her, had someone seen her that night, would she be alive? Could we have saved her by seeing her?

Or did she do it when we came back, when we were sleeping? Did the shot ring out and did we turn, each of us in our separate dreams, toward the noise?

In the dark room of myself where I ask the dangerous questions, the answers explode into pieces that are lodged into every square inch of my life.

Aᴄᴛᴇʀ I returned from Manhattan, Kevin, the history professor that I had been dating, took me out to an Italian restaurant, where he asked me about my trip to New York. That was his favorite thing, eating Italian food and talking. He wasn't a bad guy, we had some chemistry, he was not unattractive. There are worse things. And honestly, we could probably have had some semblance of a life together—there was something kitschy and downtown about shacking up with a college professor. But Gigi would have hated him for the fact that he was a financially poor intellectual who was only firming up my lower position in the social stratosphere. And I found the fact that he was into me extremely questionable—my weight was always on the uptick, and I often forgot to wash my hair for days.

But I forgot I had even mentioned the New York trip to him and was, in fact, surprised to find that I even did at all. Cross-referencing calendars implied a mutual domestication, glossy and bland, as if our lives were a plate of pasta we were now sharing.

"The trip was good," I said, after finishing my wine in one gulp. I signaled the waiter for another.

"Is your sister like you?"

He gazed at me with that soft, wanting, puppy-dog face, as if he hoped I'd see that he was attentive, considerate. *Look, I'm interested in your family*, he was saying. *Look, we have a future here.*

"No," I answered. "She bathes."

After dinner Kevin and I went back to his apartment where I drank more wine, and he continued to search in earnest for the thing that would open me to him. I spent the night, but nothing really happened besides a little touching, a lot of sleeping. Somehow I'd inadvertently led him to believe that I was waiting to see how this would play out before we went too far. He was perpetually frustrated, but in this waiting I imagined he glimpsed the prize of our future together, and in my abstinence he chose to see a jewel of tenderness, and therefore my waiting was drenched with more meaning, as if I was waiting for the perfect moment to give myself to him. He had no idea that this waiting had nothing to do with him. It was a waiting in which I always was thrusting myself backward away from him and this present as I know it, in an attempt to reverse all that's happened and force it to a standstill, where I can turn it all around.

And since he started asking me questions about my family it meant he would have to go, although I'm sure something else would have ended it even if I hadn't. He would have eventually found my elevator obsession tiring and odd instead of endearing and fun. He would have feared my insistence on always sitting two rows behind him at the movies was not an eccentric game but a strange fetish. It was nothing more than a sad ploy to watch him from the back, so that in the short time of the movie I could imagine he was my father, who needed only to turn around.

Beyond the balcony where I sit with the contents of the box, the sun is now set. I can no longer see urban sprawl, but the lights that dot it, a kind of flickering outline.

Earlier than the questions about what our father looked like were the questions about where Daddy had gone. My mother had no answer, there was no answer, any answer was circular. He was gone because he was gone. He left because he was a leaver. And he wasn't Daddy. He stopped being Daddy because he was gone.

But there was always that concern in my mother that would surface during these conversations, a deep panic, a metaphysical scrambling to leave us with something that would not haunt us for all of our days. *He's gone*, she would say, *but he left something behind that's so, so, important, even more important than him leaving.*

What? Gigi and I would ask. *What is it?* We were so excited we instantly became breathless, our heads crammed with ideas about a big wrapped present somewhere with our names on it, inside of it a bike, a dollhouse, a puppy.

He left you! Mom would squeal. *He left me three beautiful girls, and now I have you all to myself.*

We sensed in this an absence, as if we were only the trace of what had been there, the contour of an empty shape.

Later on when I was rummaging through Mom's room on a treasure hunt, I discovered she had told us a lie. We were not all he had left behind. He had also left behind something dark and not meant for me, like a secret overheard. A secret in a drawer. Something cold and heavy and metallic that I was not supposed to touch or tell about.

But I showed Lulu what I had found, proud to have discovered it, to have seen it first with my own eyes.

AFTER Lulu's death, I became terrified of stairs. Stairs became nothing but a closed door behind which there was no life, only an outline of life that signified an ascension to death, like my sister and her hippie boyfriend, two birds rising only to find they are caged, enlightened by nothing, transcending to nowhere.

I AM sitting out on my balcony with the contents of my sister Lulu's box. A patchwork quilt, two philosophy books, a volume of poetry, incense, a poster. Relics from a time I ceased to know Lulu, after she shed her popularity and gave up notions of liberating her mind with drugs and wandered into a kind of scaled-down life. It was a retreat in secret, in the same way that I retreat inside now, with the contents of the box.

Except I retreat toward a secret. The one only I know, that Lulu once saw our father. "You saw who?" I had asked, after she told me, not confident I heard her right.

"Dad," she repeated. It was strange to hear her say it. By the time we were teenagers the word *Dad* was so foreign in our house. We said things like *pop quiz* and *cotillion* and *whiskey* and *bitch* but not *Dad*. Never *Dad*. *Dad* had long since been erased from our language centers.

She saw him when she was four while reading a picture book on the couch. He came down the stairs and put his jacket on. Glanced at her. Walked out the door and never came back.

"That was it," she said. "He looked at me, knowing he was leaving, and he gave away nothing. As if I was nothing. I was as inanimate as the wall. I was a flicker of light to catch his eye. This was my first childhood memory."

Not long after that, I became a spectator to my sister as she shook off the costumes of valedictorian and prom queen and exploded into the kaleidoscope of drugs and hippie boyfriends and later descended down into the dark basement of introspection and solitude, and I wondered how a person could live so many existences, how someone might change so many times over.

But these existences were only imitations of death, a mimic of her first memory, that of being made suddenly aware of her own startling nonexistence, of her backwards birth into self-annihilation.

Aɴᴅ what is the trajectory of my own life? The answer to this question is emblematic of the problem with my novel, which is going nowhere. Truthfully, it was never a novel, but a memoir. Not a memoir, a biography of myself. Not a biography, autobiographical fiction. A poorly written diary entry, really. A memory. A dream. A confession. A vignette of a room at the top of the stairs from which I cannot seem to move.

See, in this vignette, I lay the quilt over the bed, the only cover she used in those last days, as if she welcomed the coldness, as if coldness was the final cure. Place the incense on the nightstand, where it often burned at night when she would sit on her bed and read. Stack the books on the floor and tack the poster to the wall, the one with the torn edges, hung slightly crooked, the way Lulu had hung it.

You see, that morning, my mother sent me to bring Lulu down. The door was closed, and the knock returned no answer. But I did not turn around, as I told my mother I did, as I have told you. I went through the door.

Then, the quilt, the incense, the books, the poster. Next, Lulu on the floor, leaning against the foot of her bed in last night's clothes. Sitting upright, but kind of flopped, contorted in some way I could not understand. Finally, her eyes open and staring, not at me, but slightly cast down. Finally, something I did. I kneeled down in front of her and leveled our eyes.

Can you see that scene now? Can you see it? You are the one on the balcony across the highway. You've seen me see you. Now you're up close, in the doorway. Come on, you play me, I'll play Lulu. Look at me on the floor, in front of the bed, incense burning. When you kneel down in front of me and level our eyes, I will let you into that gate, into the dark behind the dark. You have seen now what I've seen: the incense in the dish, the child on the couch, the fallen face at the table. But there is one more thing. When I pass this final thing to you, my eyes will no longer reflect it, they will become the empty pages of this book, and it will be yours to carry on, just as I have carried with me what I saw that morning, the blood-red color of Lulu's soul that had been trapped by my father's look forever inside of her, flushed out finally through the bullet hole in that sweet manner of release for which only the dead are grateful.

ONE RIGHT THING
ONE RIGHT THING

There I was at my twenty-year high school reunion in a Jersey hotel banquet room, feeling like I was in one of those dreams where you show up to the party only to realize you're not wearing pants, and you're late and, anyway, you weren't invited. This was exactly how I felt back in high school, which I thought added a nice symmetry to the whole experience.

I had brought my younger sister, Tess, whose optimism was equal parts authenticity and overcompensation. We landed at the bar, which, as usual, was the most popular real estate in the room. Tess ordered two Diet Cokes and handed me one.

"Alright," she said. "Let's make some memories. Shall we dance?"

I glanced at the wooden platform in the center of the room that held roughly twenty-four square feet of wiggling body parts. "Absolutely and indefinitely no," I said.

"I'll take that as a *maybe later*. How about we mingle?"

"Would rather be buried alive. What's option number three?"

She crossed her arms. "Stand here like an asshole and speak to no one."

"Done." I sipped my nonalcoholic carbonated drink while gazing out over the crowd. What did I have to say to these people anyway? I didn't know them. They didn't know me. We were familiar in the sense that we had endured a prolonged period of crowdedness, like being crammed into a stalled elevator with a bunch of strangers. Not in the sense that the thrust of our lives were charging parallel and forward, at the same speed, toward some similar, fantastic destination.

The reunion had been Tess's idea. I'd agreed to go a month earlier, after she'd spotted the invite in my apartment.

"It's your twenty year, Jonah," she'd said, as she followed me into the dining room with a stack of plates. Our parents were on their way for a celebratory dinner around my recent promotion at work.

"It's a bad idea," I said.

"It's a great idea. You're the troubled teenage alcoholic who's all transformed and handsome. There's so much poetry in this it's absurd."

"No one remembers me. I didn't even walk with the class."

"But now you can walk among them." She put the plates down and spread her arms out, presenting the air with palms up, her wild curly hair harnessed, in part, by crisscrossed bobby pins around the top of her head. Then she dropped her arms and sighed. "Anyway, a reunion is just a normal thing. It's healthy to do a normal thing."

Even at thirty-six she had the same look on her face that she did as a starry-eyed, watchful ten-year-old, knocking on my bedroom door, waving some CD and begging me to have a dance party in my room.

"I'll make you a deal," I said, setting forks and knives down around the table. "I'll go for one hour. Tops. And you're my date. Can you set the plates now?"

"Counteroffer," she said, not moving. "I'm your date *and* you agree to seriously consider the counseling thing at Meadow Glen."

The counseling thing was this paid internship at the rehab from which I was an alumnus. Tess worked there as a counselor. The program she was pushing would earn me a counseling certification and, mostly likely, a job at the treatment center. She had been on my ass about it for almost two years. Her tenacity was award-winning.

"I just got a promotion at work," I said. "That's why we're all celebrating tonight."

"And it's gonna be a great party. But you don't want to work in finance. Also, your silverware is wrong. Forks go on the right."

I looked down at the table. "Forks go on the left. And why do you say I don't want to work in finance?"

"No one wants to work in finance. Forks go on the right. The *R* in fork is for right, that's how you remember."

This was fishy because Tess liked to deal in dubious facts, and I'd never heard of the *R* thing. Then again, I'd spent more of my life working the AA steps than arranging cutlery for dinner parties. Plus, the last thing I needed was my mom thinking I was some inept man-child who didn't know where to put a fork.

"It's a great job," I told Tess, as I switched the silverware. "I'm beyond lucky to have ever even gotten in at entry level, let alone work my way up the ladder."

"You sound like dad. This is just a job, Jonah. Not something you can call a career. A life's work."

"Now *you* sound like dad. Can you set the plates?"

She glared at me. "You have to put the napkins down first. They go under the plate."

Another questionable fact, but once again I couldn't really trust my instinct when it came to a thing like proper napkin coordinates, so I did as Tess said. When I finished, she was still standing at the plates, as if holding them hostage.

"Fine," I said. "I'll consider the counseling thing. Now can you please set the plates?"

"*Seriously* consider it. And I'll be your date to the reunion. Just think of the poetry."

Then she left the room, leaving me to set the plates.

IF there was any poetry in this hotel banquet room, it certainly wasn't in the banners plastered about with exclamatory phrases like *Welcome Back Class of '94!* Nor was there any poetry in the way I stood out among the throng of alumni doubled by their plus-ones, all done up in suits and ties and sparkly cocktail dresses, white name tags affixed over hearts as if proudly announcing these grown-up versions of their young, spirited selves. My nametag was slapped over a brown blazer, no tie, my blondish curls turned full mop, as if I was announcing nothing more than the presence of the grown-out version of my young, straggly self.

My teenage years were christened by a terrible uncertainty about not only where my space was in the world but *if* a space even existed for me. The kind of metaphysical misgivings that gave way to drinking and suicidal ideation, during which I made a grand discovery: I didn't care about a metaphysical anything as long as you kept the drinks coming. The consolation prize for such a discovery was entry into rehab at the beginning of senior year; after being deemed dry by the institution, I returned to school only to feel even more of an outsider, so I finished school at home, did a couple stints in a halfway house, and then moved into an efficiency with peeling paint, a mattress on the floor, a beat-up Goodwill couch, and a large, questionable stain on the wall which, I thought, really tied it all together. It was a special place, that squalor of sobriety.

My first slip was on my twenty-third birthday. Tess surprised me with balloons and a cake at my efficiency. I surprised her with the six pack of beer in my hand.

I didn't intend to drink the beer, necessarily. I just wanted to be a normal guy, picking up a sixer after work. I felt, in some way, like I deserved a little normalcy. My five years of sobriety had culminated in a mindless telemarketing job my dad's friend had given me, weekly AA meetings, and ramen-noodle dinners in front of basic cable.

You know, the sober life. The happier, hobbled, sober life.

"What exactly are you going to do with that?" Tess asked me, pointing at the beer from the middle of the room. She was twenty-one and luminous, a kind of supernova just appearing on the horizon.

"I don't know. I just wanted to have it."

"This is a spectacularly bad idea, Jonah," she said as she set the cake on the counter and stationed the weighted balloons by the TV.

"Could be worse. Could be just a regularly bad idea."

"Oh, it's that too. You've successfully covered every form of bad idea." She thrust her hand at me. "Give me the beer."

"No," I said, my hand gripping the carrier. "I just want to have it in here with me."

"You should call your sponsor."

"He can get his own."

"That is not funny," Tess said. "That is not funny at all."

I stared at her, not moving. She stared back. Underneath, I felt addiction trying to deflate the life raft of sobriety in which I'd been floating.

Tess was the first to break the standoff. "You do know that consuming alcohol after a five-year dry spell can send your system into acute ethylphylactic intoxication shock. You could die."

"That's not a thing," I said, although, by the way she said it, it really did seem like a thing. With her it *always* sounded like a thing. I found myself actually wondering if death by ethyl-whatever was quick and painless or slow and grueling.

She gave me an it's-your-funeral look and calmly popped the top off the cake's plastic container. "We are still going to celebrate your birth. You will not open that six pack in my presence. You will eat cake and marinate on the fact that sobriety is the better way."

We ate in silence, the beer watching from the counter like an uninvited guest. She took her time by slowly savoring not one, not two, but three helpings of cake, probably hoping to time out any imminent relapse. After the third piece of cake she left, but not before she hugged me and told me she loved me no matter what.

I held out for a day and then went for the bottle opener, which I realized Tess had swiped. Small victory. But eventually I found my way into that beer and settled nicely into my relapse.

STANDING near an open bar and avoiding interaction at the reunion was turning out to be a big fat lesson in futility. I was forced to field passing *hello Jonahs* and *how are you Jonahs* that were obviously prompted by my nametag. Eventually a petite woman in a bright-blue cocktail dress stopped right in front of me, presumably for a more prolonged exchange.

"Jonah Cavanaugh!" she exclaimed, holding a drink in one hand and a plate of food in the other. Her nametag read *Nina*. She had a melting, weepy look, as if we were long-lost friends, reunited. I had no idea who she was.

"You look great!" she said, nodding enthusiastically while examining me.

"Thanks," I managed. "Likewise."

"What in the world have you been up to?" she asked.

"Oh, just wasting time," I said. "Sitting on the dock of the bay."

Tess elbowed me while Nina adopted a little frown.

"I'm trying to remember," Nina said. "Did you transfer senior year?"

"Sort of." I looked sideways at Tess.

"I'm Tess," she jumped in. "Jonah's sister."

Nina nodded at Tess for a moment and then was back to me, whom she was clearly desperate to place. "Where did you transfer to?"

"Meadow Glen," I said.

Nina nodded again, but her face had gone blank.

"It's a treatment center," Tess added.

"Treatment center?" Nina asked.

"Rehab," I conceded.

Nina processed this information while focusing on my Diet Coke. Which is precisely when the single, five-watt light bulb in her brain flickered on.

"*Right. Rehab.*" She was back to nodding again, but this time it was slow and deliberate, as if the delicate subject matter warranted special nodding.

"How about you?" Tess asked. "What have you been up to?"

Big smile. This was clearly her favorite question ever. "Married to an investment banker. Five kids. We've got such a full house! We have to keep moving just to fit everyone!"

"I know what you mean," I said, as the conversation hit a heavy pause. "About feeling crowded."

Her smile dimmed as she shifted her weight.

Tess gestured toward Nina's plate. "Well, we don't want to keep you."

"Right. Well great to see you! We should dance later?"

"Can't," I said, indicating the general area of my leg. "Speed-boating injury."

"He's kidding," Tess said. "Dancing sounds great."

Nina nodded unsurely while moving away. I rattled the ice around in my glass.

"Well," Tess said, not looking at me. "You certainly got the asshole part down."

WHEN I was thirty I moved into my first apartment alone after living with various AA buddies. It had been three years since a second relapse and yet another return to rehab. By then I'd eked my way through college courses online and made it out with a business degree. My dad had used yet another connection to get me a job in finance that paid more and offered perks like vacation days and bonuses. I was dating a senior in college named Dana, whom I met at the Dollar Theater six months earlier.

Tess had come over to help me unpack. We were in the bedroom, on the floor, going through boxes. She opened one, pulling out some loose socks.

"This is how you packed your socks? None of these are paired, Jonah."

"Can you pair them and put them in the drawer? And make sure you leave the left side of the dresser empty for Dana."

"Why?"

"Because she's moving in."

I opened a box that was only half full with a few pairs of shoes, some sweaters, and miscellaneous bathroom stuff.

"Here?" Tess asked. "No, the 7-Eleven down the street. Yes, here. I already told you this."

"Does she need to get permission from her RA?"

I looked up at her. She was digging through the socks, looking unusually sullen. "What's wrong with you? Things going sour with Ryan?"

"We broke up. He stole my gerbil."

"You have a gerbil?"

"I *had* a gerbil."

"That's weird."

"What is? That I had a gerbil or that he stole it?"

"Both."

She shrugged, tossing a pair of socks into the drawer. "Although it's possible I planted it in his apartment so I could accuse him of stealing it and break up with him."

"That's even weirder."

"I know."

There was a look on her face. That kind of adult bewilderment. When you realize the world is no different then when you were a kid, you're just privy to how little you understand it.

"She's not in the program," Tess said.

"What? Who?" I was still thinking about the gerbil thing.

"Dana. She's not in the program."

I'd dated several girls from the program, all based on a formula—an artificial bond over chain-smoking and recycled stories about drinking. Dana was just a normal human being who had no stories about getting drunk in the locker-room showers before school or vomiting in a convenience store after a drunken late-night run for Cheetos.

"I'm tired of girls in the program," I said, opening another half-full box of some unfolded towels. "It's too much of the same. It just feels like I'm dating myself."

Now she looked deeply concerned, as if we were discussing the matter of my grave illness. "She's so young Jonah. She hasn't been where you've been."

"How unfortunate that she hasn't had to detox, twice, in a state hospital and transition back into society alongside recovering crack addicts who can't see their kids."

"But that's my point. She can't possibly understand the gravity of your experiences."

"I think that's a plus," I answered, my good mood sliding toward a cramped, smothered feeling. "She hasn't been eroded by a bunch of hard ideas about life. She's laid back. She's fun."

"Too fun. Too laid back. And not enough hard ideas."

I threw up my hands. "Can we not talk about this? How did we even get here?"

"I just think that living with her is a dangerous proposition," she insisted. "She represents all the old things for you. Late nights and parties and unbridled freedom. That lifestyle could easily be a trigger for you to slip."

"With that kind of language there certainly is no confusion as to what you do for a living. I'll be fine, Tess."

We fell into a silence as she paired and tossed socks, and I opened a few more boxes half full with random stuff. It was dawning on me for the first time that I didn't own much. It seemed by thirty I should have acquired enough things to fill more than a few boxes. Maybe that was part of the reason why I wanted Dana to move in, to fill up my drawers with things, to make up for all I didn't have, although I couldn't see it at the time. Nor could I see that Tess was right; I was headed for a relapse in just a few months, another reset on the old clock of sobriety.

But at the time I insisted privately I was fine. While figuring out where to put my smattering of things, I eventually realized I was alone, Tess having left to watch TV in the other room. I went over to the drawer to check her work. She'd paired every sock, alright, just not with their matching pair.

Tess and I arrived at the buffet table, where we filled our plates with too many foods from too many genres and then stood at the edge of the dining area, scanning the seating situation. The empty table toward the back was the obvious choice but Tess was already headed toward a table full of people. I followed, once again, reluctantly. We sat down and Tess chatted up the table while I ate quietly over my plate. There was a group of five women, best friends throughout high school, all of them divorced and still the best of friends. Across the table was a couple who had been together since freshman year but broke up after graduation and found other partners, only to split and find each other again. I recognized them from the mosh-pit part of my memory where I tossed all high school couples with their excessive hand-holding and endless canoodling-by-the-locker. But I had to admit they possessed a real glow, a quiet happiness, the kind you arrive at humbly through surrender to a second-chance life that's only possible when you admit you failed at the first one. Everyone at the table had that glow, except me. Even Tess had it, in her old-soul kind of way.

"Listen," she said, leaning in very close to me as the table broke out into smaller discussions. "I can get you out of here."

"You can?" I asked, lowering my ear to her as I tried to stab a tiny eggroll.

"Yep." She gestured toward the dance floor with her fork. "But we can only escape through the dance floor. You're gonna have to dance your way out of here."

I checked out the dance floor, where the excessive wiggling raged on. I cringed.

"Can we go through the air vent instead?"

"Oh my God," she said.

"Fine, we'll dig a tunnel through the subfloor. *Again.*"

"No," she said, pushing my chin with her finger toward a large man, tall and pushing rotund, accosting an enormous plate of food a couple of tables over.

"What?" I asked. "Who is that?"

"That's James Nolan," she said, incredulous. "Quarterback and hottest guy in school. Maybe ever. But now . . .I can't even believe it."

I couldn't even believe it either. This was a guy I used to envy—tons of swagger, no trace of any metaphysical misgivings. He was hunched low over his plate and was completely alone. From here it seemed he certainly didn't have any happy glow, unless you counted the pile of glistening buttered rolls that was reflecting onto his face. Which made me wonder, did I get what I wanted, to be like James Nolan, only not in the way I'd wanted it? Were both of us now marooned by whatever overeating and overdrinking and general disappointment had led us to a lackluster and lonely life?

Two years earlier Tess treated me to breakfast-for-dinner at our favorite diner. She had big news she wanted to share.

"I took a job at the rehab," she said, after our waffles had arrived. "*Your* rehab. Isn't it funny how things are circular?"

"Yeah, like a hamster wheel."

"Depressing! How about like the earth? Or like a ballerina in a music box? Anyway, I'm running the internship program and I have a great idea. You should intern at the center. It's paid and you can get your counseling certification."

"I have a job," I said, as I took a sip of my coffee and watched her butter her waffles like she was icing a cake.

"You mean that bogus finance job you got through yet another one of Dad's friends? Please. You're dying inside, I can see it. You should think about the internship. It's a chance to really make an impact in people's lives. People who need it. You know a thing or two about that."

What did I know, actually? I knew about relapses. I knew about taking yet another job my dad had found for me. I knew about the world becoming larger and more complicated the longer I was in it, as if I was shrinking. And of course I knew more people than I should have in the diner from the myriad meetings that made every day feel like a floating, isolated thing, never adding up to anything significant.

"What does Kyle think about you counseling drunks and junkies?" I asked.

"Who?"

"Your boyfriend?"

"Collin," she corrected.

"Oh," I said, looking into my coffee, feeling like a jerk. More evidence that I knew very little about not much. Especially about Tess. I had been so in and out in my own life—just when I was in, I'd screw up, then I was out, back at Camp Sobriety, learning how to walk and talk again, like some perpetual stroke victim. In all of that time, Tess's life had moved on and on and on, and I couldn't even hang on to the name of one important person in her life.

"Well, are you and Collin gonna tie the knot?" I asked, trying to recover.

She rolled her eyes. "It's only been six months, Jonah. Give it a minute."

"Right," I said, watching as she forked some waffles into her mouth.

"Hey," she said, after swallowing a few bites. "You should go swing dancing with me and Collin. Tuesday nights. It's fun."

"Swing dancing? Fun? I don't know any of the words you're saying right now."

"Yes, swing dancing. You really should come. It was Collin's idea."

"Oh yeah, why?" I asked roughly.

"Why was that his idea?" She dropped her fork heavily down on the plate. "Gee, I don't know. For the irony? Or maybe to get to know you, genius."

I was painfully aware of the difference between being a person worth knowing and a person someone else thinks is worth knowing. The latter holding imminent disappointment that I didn't wish on any poor soul, not even Collin.

"Tell you what," I said. "We'll skip the formality. Give me his address and I'll just send him a fruit basket."

She looked at me for a long beat. "Are you serious?"

"Yeah. He doesn't need to waste his time."

"Him? Or you?"

"I don't know. Both? More him though."

"So is this your gig?" she asked, sitting back in the seat and crossing her arms. She still had that watchful look, but it was more jaded, less starry-eyed.

"What do you mean, *my gig*?"

"You know—I'm disappointed so you're disappointed. Cosmic loner projecting his disappointment on everyone else. It's a great ideology. Hope for nothing and all will be fulfilled."

"I have no idea what you're talking about. There's no gig. There's just one day at a time."

"Spare me." She pushed her plate away, I assumed for effect, which was working. I'd seen a lot of deep frustration from Tess but never so much that she might give up.

"Look, is this about the dancing? I'll think about it, OK?"

"No you won't. Just like you're not gonna think about the internship, which could be great for you. You're just gonna think about your after-care treatment, which is great. You don't ever have to actually move on."

I went to speak but was tongue-tied by a burning indignation. Easy for her to ruminate on the private and complex world of the alcoholic. She had no clue, I thought, about recovery. But before I could get any of that out, she had already stood and left the diner, somehow swiping my cigarettes and leaving me with the check.

A FEW more people stopped by the table and said *hello*, some of whom I remembered vaguely, but most of whom I did not. I noticed several folks had joined James Nolan's table, and they all seemed to be chatting amiably. This gave me a strange relief even if his clearly long-gone six-pack and chiseled shoulders were still unsettling me. I certainly didn't wish the plight of the outsider on anyone. After I'd cleaned my plate, I left Tess inside at the table and went outside to smoke. There was a small group of people who had just finished their cigarettes and were now coming inside; a lone woman stayed behind to smoke another cigarette. She was wearing a short, black dress and black combat boots, hair a mass of curls. From here she sort of looked like an edgy version of our class president, one person I did remember, mostly because of the random fact that her headbands always perfectly matched her sweaters *and* her notebooks.

"Hi," she said, as I joined her at the ashtray. She glanced indiscreetly at my nametag. "Jonah."

She was not wearing a nametag. I stalled.

"Amelia," she said, pointing to the place her nametag would have been.

"It *is* you," I said.

"It is?"

"Class president."

"Please," she said, "do not remind me that I was a total asshole."

"That doesn't sound like something the class president would say. What happened to your school spirit?"

She raised her eyebrows. "Well that's long gone. I'm into kicking puppies and generally being in a foul mood."

"Well I dig the boots. Very good for puppy-kicking."

She nodded a few times. "I dig your lack of tie."

I dipped my head in a *thank you* and took a drag. She took one too. This moment of leveling was most unexpected—me sharing a smoke with the class president.

"So," she said. "What about you? Marriage and kids and jobs and cars?"

"Did you just list a bunch of nouns?"

"Sorry, I'm not very good at this. I think I'm supposed to ask you what you're up to these days or something?"

"Oh, well, no marriage, no kids. I do have a job and a car. I brought my sister Tess as my date tonight."

"No shit," she said, laughing. "I brought mine too. Corinne. Well, sister-in-law. Ex-sister-in-law. She actually went to school here, but we didn't even meet until after we both divorced our husbands, who were brothers. This is getting more depressingly weird, the more I say it out loud."

Now this made me laugh. She laughed again too.

"Anyway, she's my wingman," Amelia said. "We're like the Wingmen of Weirdness."

"Sounds about right," I said. "Honestly, I don't even know why I'm here."

"For the pain. And the buffet."

"It's just—what's the point of a reunion if I'm not actually *reuniting* with anyone? No one in there remembers me and quite frankly, I don't remember them."

"You're lucky. I'm trying to *forget* everyone. And get everyone to do the same." She was laughing again.

"You were that bad, huh?"

"I was just clueless, that's all. Young Me thought that when life gives you lemons you just hold a pep rally. But I guess that's the point. We're supposed to grow up and shudder at our young selves."

"What if you haven't changed and you're shuddering at your young self *and* your adult self? What if it's just one long shuddering at yourself in perpetuity?"

"I don't know. I think that's everyone. Everyone sucks and should be shuddering at themselves. But at least you know you suck, right? I think that may be the only way you stand a chance of becoming a decent person."

I thought about James Nolan, how I'd watched him engage nicely with the people that eventually joined his table. I couldn't recall James ever doing anything nicely, unless you considered harassing girls or shoving guys around in the hall as friendly exchanges. Maybe I'd been wrong in my earlier assessment of him as lifeless and lonely; maybe things were somehow better for him *because* the life had been sucked out of him a little bit.

"Anyway," Amelia went on, "my advice is, don't be so hard on yourself. You don't look so bad to me."

She ashed her cigarette, one arm under her elbow, and I thought, *She's flirting*. But then again, she just seemed like a person who didn't avoid a glance and told things straight.

"Speaking of not looking bad," she said. "Have you seen Gigi Martin? She's all black pantsuit, serious New York City ad exec now. The teachers couldn't get her to wear *enough* clothing when we were in school. No one would have bet on her."

I shook my head, trying to place Gigi Martin. Nothing.

"Her older sister was the prom queen who committed suicide the summer after we graduated," Amelia added.

"That's *right*," I said, a deep memory shaking itself from the kelp, that of hearing the news of the suicide while I was back at the halfway house. It had been shocking then, and to be reminded of it now gave me that odd leveling feeling for the second time tonight.

"Is it wrong to say that at least we made it this far?" I asked.

"No. It's just true," she said. We shared a couple of quiet drags. Then she tossed her cigarette. "I better get back inside."

"Yes," I said, glancing at my watch. "I gotta get back to my sister."

This got her cracking up again. We walked toward the entrance.

"Challenge," she said. "Tonight you do one thing that would make Young You shudder."

"Like what?"

"How would I know? Only you know that. That's the point. It can be something small. Then you can say with certainty you're not exactly the same person you were before."

We entered the banquet room, stopping in the doorway.

"A toast," I said, turning toward her and raising an invisible glass, "to sisters."

"And the one thing," she said, raising her own invisible drink.

AFTER my parents arrived at my apartment for the celebratory dinner the night Tess and I struck the deal to go to the reunion, we took our seats at the table, passing Chinese takeout boxes around and dumping foods on our plates.

"This looks great, honey," my mom said, as if I'd actually cooked the meal. "But your silverware is on the wrong side."

I glared at Tess, who pretended to concentrate on an eggroll.

"Well, I, for one, am proud," my dad said. "You finally carved out a career, son. Not just a job."

He gripped his glass and launched his favorite speech about my role as a functional member of society. The speech included his favorite phrases like *solid trajectory* and *business acumen* and *fast track to success*. I think he was even crying a little. He really was proud and most likely terrified over what I might do next to screw it all up. Mom too, with her gentle admonishment of the table setting, even if that was a bum rap. They had done a good job for two people who really had no clue as to what to do with me.

But what parents actually know what to do with their kids? Parenting seemed like one big crapshoot that, if you're lucky, you don't even live long enough to see the outcome.

Tess ate her kung pao chicken across the table, listening absently. At that moment, I had a very old memory of her visiting me in rehab when she was fifteen. The memory contained a vividness most of my memories had lost: Tess asking me, her face big with a worry she probably thought she was hiding, whether drugs were the problem. I told her that drugs were *a* problem but not *the* problem. *The* problem was underneath. At the time *the* problem eluded me, and honestly it still did now, but since then I'd come to understand that it had a little something to do with the feeling that I just had nothing to offer.

And it was true—after all this time, I didn't have anything to offer, certainly not in the world of finance. Which is when I found myself actually holding up my part of the deal and considering the counseling thing—seriously considering it.

Dad's speech had concluded, and he was holding up his glass. "Here's to the future."

Mom raised her glass, and I followed suit, and finally Tess, with a roll of her eye only I caught.

"This is just all so delicious," Mom declared, after we'd clinked glasses around the table. "But where are the napkins?"

BACK in the banquet hall the music had switched to a slow song, and Amelia was out on the dance floor with a blonde waif of a woman who I guessed was the ex-sister-in-law. They were doing this mock slow-dance that was making them giggle uncontrollably and in turn causing a lot of disgusted stares, but those two didn't care at all. In fact, it was making them laugh more. They were totally unencumbered by embarrassment.

Because whatever happened here, it didn't matter. Amelia would go home, and the dirty looks on the dance floor would burn up like a dying star and leave nothing but a bright memory of this evening she spent just doing her thing.

I turned to Tess, who was watching the scene with amused interest. My sister who wanted to dance. Who had *always* wanted to dance, with me. It was such a small thing to want. What kind of a person was I that I couldn't grant such a small thing? Plus, maybe this was my one thing that would make Young Me die out of sheer embarrassment.

I stood up and walked over to Tess and offered my hand. She put her hand in mine, cautiously. I led her to the edge of the dance floor, which was the furthest I was comfortable going, where I put my hand to her waist, and she put hers to my shoulder.

She didn't say a word, as if that could undo this unexpected moment. I tried to lead the dance, shifting awkwardly from one foot to the next out on the dance floor.

"So how is Collin?" I asked.

Her gaze shifted beyond mine, and she tilted her head toward her shoulder in a kind of suspended shrug. "We broke up."

"What?" I asked, stopping the dance. "When?"

She sighed and pulled us back into our stilted toggle. "A few weeks ago."

"So what happened?"

"He asked me to marry him."

"That pig."

"I know, I know. He was so earnest about it. That's what kills me. I told him it wasn't him, it was me. As in literally me—I told him I'm a gamophobe."

"What's a gamophobe?"

"Someone who has a fear of marriage. I said that just talking about it could render me neurogenically immobile."

"No. Did he buy that?"

She smirked. *Yep*, I thought, *he probably did.*

"So no marriage at all or just no marriage to Collin?"

"I don't know." Her blue eyes moved over the dance floor, serious and distant. "Not sure it's my way. Don't tell Dad. I hate it when he cries."

"Why isn't it your way?"

"I don't know. I think I'm built for something else."

"Like what?"

"Working at the rehab, is one." She looked at me while settling a grip more firmly on my shoulders. "And keeping you out of trouble."

"That could be a full-time job."

"Tell me about it. When you first came back from rehab way back when, I rode my bike to that supermarket where you worked, and I spied on you."

"You did?"

She looked away again. "Yeah. I went in and pretended to shop. I even asked a lady for soup recommendations to make the ruse more real."

"You're always pulling a fast one," I said. "What is that about?"

She shrugged. "You don't hold the monopoly on rebellion."

I generally saw Tess as together, unshakable, confident. But she was also the Tess who told tall tales and had sticky fingers and was always slipping out the back door when it came to relationships. Because being a person was just a bare-knuckled scrap for survival. We were the same, I guess, in a way that couldn't be any more different, in that way that everyone is a weird and private mystery unto themselves.

It seemed the right moment to tell her that I'd considered the counseling thing and was gonna go for it. But the song was changing to a fast one, and Tess was pulling away from me, knowing our time on the dance floor had run its course. But I held on to her, keeping her there. I wanted to stay here. Something about staying with my sister, who had been watching me with a vigilance across the lonely sky of her entire life. She'd always been my wingman. And even though the slow dance had accomplished the one thing that would have mortified a younger me, it didn't feel quite right.

I started to sway slowly to the song, pulling Tess along. She tilted her head, confused. People were cramming onto the dance floor. Then I put a little groove in it and picked up speed before pushing off from her into some full-blown ridiculous moves I had no idea were inside of me. Tess didn't miss a step joining in, laughing, loving this.

Maybe that was it, I thought, as we got down on the dance floor, not just one thing I would have done, but the one right thing that had been there all along, me inhabiting a place inside Tess's heart, among its constellation of precious things. How lucky I was to live there. How lucky to be loved for nothing at all except who you are in your own lovely troubled being.

Acknowledgments

Thanks to the editors of *Beloit Fiction Journal,* who published "Halfway House," and *Michigan Quarterly Review,* which published "Smells Like Leslie Gray Martin."

Thank you to the people who have helped me when I've been up, down, and sideways, including:

Ben Furnish and the staff at BkMk Press, who have been so supportive and terrific and straight-up awesome. This book could not have found a better home.

Amy Wallen, who has been a tireless reader of my work. I'd be in a ditch right now without you as a writing partner, joke-dealer, and, above all else, friend.

Ben Loory and Jim Shepard, the titans of writing, who not only graciously read my work but said such nice things about it I might have cried.

Clint McCown, who taught me how to write. This collection would not be here today without your insight, guidance, honesty, and unwavering belief in me.

Ellen Lesser and David Jauss, whose early feedback was critical to the success of these stories.

My mom and dad, who long ago gave me my first StarWriter Word Processor and told me to go hog wild.

Jonathan Groves, who has been my rock, my vanguard, my advocate. You taught me that integrity and workmanship are the most important things as a writer—and that all else is vanity. You bring meaning and joy to my days.

Rachel Groves is a graduate of SMU and the Vermont College of Fine Arts MFA program. Her fiction has appeared in *Beloit Fiction Journal*, *Michigan Quarterly Review*, and elsewhere. *When We Were Someone Else* is her first book. A New Jersey native and current resident of Dallas, Texas, she has also lived in Kansas City, Missouri.

Winners of the
G. S. Sharat Chandra Prize for Short Fiction:

A Bed of Nails by Ron Tanner,
selected by Janet Burroway

I'll Never Leave You by H. E. Francis,
selected by Diane Glancy

The Logic of a Rose: Chicago Stories by Billy Lombardo,
selected by Gladys Swan

Necessary Lies by Kerry Neville Bakken,
selected by Hilary Masters

Love Letters from a Fat Man by Naomi Benaron,
selected by Stuart Dybek

Tea and Other Ayama Na Tales by Eleanor Bluestein,
selected by Marly Swick

Dangerous Places by Perry Glasser,
selected by Gary Gildner

Georgic by Mariko Nagai,
selected by Jonis Agee

Living Arrangements by Laura Maylene Walter,
selected by Robert Olen Butler

Garbage Night at the Opera by Valerie Fioravanti,
selected by Jacquelyn Mitchard

Boulevard Women by Lauren Cobb,
selected by Kelly Cherry

Thorn by Evan Morgan Williams,
selected by Al Young

King of the Gypsies by Lenore Myka,
selected by Lorraine M. López

Heirlooms by Rachel Hall,
selected by Marge Piercy

The Owl That Carries Us Away by Doug Rams,
selected by Billy Lombardo

When We Were Someone Else by Rachel Groves,
selected by Hilma Wolitzer